BLUE RIVER

ALSO BY ETHAN CANIN

Emperor of the Air

BLUE RIVER

ETHAN CANIN

HOUGHTON
MIFFLIN
COMPANY
BOSTON

For information about permission to reproduce selections
from this book, write to Permissions, Houghton Mifflin
Company, 2 Park Street, Boston, Massachusetts 02108.

Library of Congress Cataloging-in-Publication Data

Canin, Ethan.
    Blue river   /   Ethan Canin.
        p.   cm.
    ISBN 0-395-49854-6
    I. Title.
    PS3553.A495B58   1991
    813'.54 — dc20   91-16565
                                    CIP

Printed in the United States of America

BP 10 9 8 7 6 5 4 3 2

"I have never heard of a crime which I could not imagine committing myself."

— Goethe

BLUE RIVER

Prologue

As a boy my brother Lawrence was always hiding. He hid behind doors, under porches, in the deep shade of trees; he lay down in drainage ditches and fields of tall grass and fell asleep; he submerged himself in the Mississippi River and breathed through a short length of reed while the other boys and girls played tag on the shore. In the afternoons I was sent to find him for dinner. I was five years old the first time I went to look for him; that day he was sleeping in our back yard behind a cut stump. Later I would find him crawling in the heating duct in our basement, squatting on the limb of our maple with his head in the leaves, standing in our yard in a hole he had dug deeper than his head. I was always coming across him by surprise. In our house he walked noiselessly. He sat in the corners of rooms. He was six years older than I was, and I regarded him with reverence. One April afternoon when it had been drizzling for days he walked to the shore of the Mississippi, lay down on the beach, and covered himself up to his neck in the sand. I found him there when I was sent to fetch him for dinner, smiling slightly, just his head showing, his face turned up to the spring rain.

Then, when he was in high school, he stopped hiding. His voice grew louder, his step became pronounced, and he began roaming about the world in the open. He fought; he stole; he came home drunk, knocking over the maple coat rack in our front hall. All the time I expected him to be standing in the corners of rooms or squatting in trees or lying in the tall grass at the back of fields. I didn't think anyone ever changed like that. But now he had a closet full of stolen clothes and a real set of brass knuckles between the box spring and mattress of his bed; he came home in police cruisers. More than once I found his shirt soaking in our bathroom, settled blood darkening the bottom of the sink. A white scar crossed the knuckles of his right hand; one eyelid drooped. He slid open the window of the bedroom we shared so his girlfriends could climb inside, their bracelets jingling in the night.

And then, the year he graduated from high school, he changed again. It happened in one day, his eighteenth birthday. After that he stopped fighting and stopped staying out until morning with his friends. He cut his hair; he moved out of our room into an apartment in the basement of our house, where he spent every night reading. He went to night school and learned engineering. He volunteered at the fire department and at the youth group of which I was a member, leading us on picnics in the state parks and flower-planting expeditions at the home for old people. At our meetings he spoke to us about discipline. From my seat in the basement of St. Vitus Church I looked up at him standing at the podium, his voice keen and his eyes filled with a fierceness that made his heart seem true and unbendable at last.

I

CALIFORNIA

ON A SUNDAY MORNING in the June of my thirty-first year I open the front door of our house looking for the newspaper and find a man standing out there: stoop-shouldered, bent, blotch-skinned, his hair and beard tangled, staring with the big, wet eyes of an animal. Some kind of bum, I think, stepping back, half-shutting the door, until I recognize him.

He stands on our porch, not moving. Not moving, I stand inside. In his gloved hand he holds the paper I have come out to find, bright from the morning sun. I have to squint, and he, though he faces the dark inside our house, squints back. Because I cannot think of what else to do I reach to take the newspaper, which he hands to me. This is something, at least — but still, he does not step inside. We have seen each other only once in fifteen years. But this is no product of coincidence — God forgive us — and what I think in that moment is that we both know this. I motion him in. He complies, his shoulders still stooped, his walk a little flop-limbed, as if the arms don't know what the legs are doing. He ducks through the doorway, although he is not tall enough to have to, and stops in our hall at the edge of the rug. The rug is of decent quality, a hand-tied Oriental, and his boots are caked with dry mud. We look at each other. Jonathan, I think to myself, is upstairs in his room.

So we stand here, he in his half-animal's pose, I in the beige, long-sleeve pajamas I wear now. They put me at a disadvantage, but by crossing my arms I try to hide their flannel monogram. At this, he bends his head forward, a polite gesture. His dark eyes blink in the weak light of the ceiling fixture; his crooked nose swells and contracts with his breaths. I see immediately that his clothing is too small, as though he has grown since buying it, like a child again somehow, outstripping his cotton pants. His ankles show above his socks.

We stand here, he looking at me and I at him. He moves his mouth occasionally as if there is a gumball in it, although there is not: I know well enough what this means. We don't speak. His knees, bony as I remember them, protrude, and even through the pants I can see the big flat patellae quivering. His breaths whistle.

My wife, Elizabeth, comes to the kitchen doorway then, wearing her own flannel pajamas, hugging her arms against the morning chill. Elizabeth is a generous woman — more generous than I — and although I do not always understand this generosity I am always grateful for it. She has never seen him except in pictures, but as we stand across from each other in our little hallway, I on the carpet and he at its rim, she comes in, strides across the room, and they embrace. She reaches up to kiss his cheek and he bends down.

"Well, Jesus," I say, "Lawrence."

"Edward," he says.

I step forward and reach my arms around him, and he reaches his own around me. They are stiffer than I remember, those arms, and firm in an unmuscled way, as if they have been cooked. We embrace. His shirt smells pungent — chlorine, I think for a moment: Has he washed it in a swimming pool?

"We've got to clean you up," says Elizabeth. She has been cooking in the kitchen, and now she wipes her hand on her pajama top, touches Lawrence's flannel shirt and glances at her finger, as though to find dust there. I married her for this frankness.

"Have breakfast with us," I say, taking his elbow to lead him to the kitchen.

"I'm hungry," he answers.

In the kitchen the skylight sun illuminates us. His skin has the pale cast of an anemic's, and on his face just below the cheekbone I notice a scratch. But I don't want to examine him like this: I motion him to the table. Our kitchen is a suburban one, made mostly of wood-colored Formica, with recessed lighting on the ceiling and a line of pictures on the free wall — small, wood-framed drawings of plants and insects. Elizabeth has hung them there and we have learned the names of all the local life. On the countertop sits a wicker basket full of green and red vegetables. Elizabeth sets down my mushroom-and-cheese omelette in front of Lawrence. She had been working on it just before he came, while I swept the pool deck and back patio. She excuses herself and goes upstairs, and Lawrence leans forward and takes a bite the size of a hamburger. The last time I saw him, five years ago in a veterans' hospital in Texas, I thought I might never see him again.

"So," I say.

Over the plate, his head is still when he chews, the thin jaw working independently. He has a beard, a mustache and thick eyebrows. He has hair in his ears.

"How've you been, Lawrence?"

"I'm fine now," he says. "I've had my troubles." He takes

another bite of the omelette and pours himself more orange juice. "I'm working," he says.

"Working where?"

The scratch reddens. He looks at me, blinking. "Jeez," he says, snorting, showing me his big teeth, which to my surprise are still white enough. "I don't remember where."

I get up from the table. There are dishes in the sink, and I step around behind him and begin washing them.

"You're a doctor," he says.

"An ophthalmologist."

"That's good." He pours another glass of orange juice. "I saw your pool."

"I work hard."

"I work hard, too."

I scrub the pan Elizabeth has cooked his eggs in. The sponge is coming apart in my hands, but I stand here anyway, tearing it up, because from the sink, behind Lawrence's back, I can watch him. Except for that day in Texas, I had last seen him when I was fifteen. He looks thin. I hear Elizabeth moving about upstairs, getting ready to come down with Jonathan. "We have a son, you know," I say.

He wipes his mouth. "Jonathan."

"He's five. We were planning to go to the zoo with him today."

"I won't stay long."

"I didn't mean that."

Elizabeth comes down the stairs with him then. Jonathan is still a shy boy, when most of his playmates are not. This troubles me a little. I cannot see where it comes from, for his mother is not shy, and, although I used to be, I don't think I am anymore. At home he sits on his windowsill a lot, looking into the rhododendron bush that has climbed up the wall outside his room. At school, when I come to pick him up, he is usually standing by himself at the edge of a group of boys. Elizabeth says not to worry, that worry only makes a child worse.

When Jonathan sees Lawrence he shifts over and stands behind the table. "Jon," I say, "come meet your uncle."

Jonathan stands with his hands in his pockets.

"Sweet Jonathan," says Elizabeth, "Uncle Lawrence wants to say hi to you."

Still he stays behind the table, looking straight ahead. "Jonathan's a little shy today," I say to Lawrence, though as my son stands there half hiding beyond the furthermost red-oak leaf of our kitchen table, I am nothing but grateful for his shyness. I turn back to the sink, grip the iron pan, and am looking down into it when I hear a noise behind me. It is wooden, the sound of something brittle, as though a chair has fallen and not, as I find when I turn around, my brother Lawrence. He lies in a heap on the floor. Jonathan, still behind the table, stares. I step over. Lawrence is limp, eyes closed, arms at angle, his long mane of hair spread across the vinyl tiles. I squat beside him and at that moment Jonathan makes a sharp inhalation — the noise of an adult, I think at once — a noise of loss. I look quickly at him, then back at my brother. His eyes blink open. The irises roll skyward. "Lawrence," I say. "Don't do this to me."

He springs up and begins cock-walking around the kitchen. His long legs move in every direction, kicking forward from the knee and out from the hip, full of gears and struts, his pants caught over his pale, hairy knees and his bony shins flying. He zigzags across the vinyl tiles, bumping into the table and chairs, knocking open the undersink cabinet, until Jonathan, laughing — *laughing!* — comes over to him. Then Lawrence leans forward and kisses him on the small, shining top of his head.

A little bit about our house, to start: some might call it luxurious, but I will not apologize for this. By the standards of the neighborhood it is not large. We had it built ourselves, the year my training ended, during a time of optimism. I used to steal away from my new office to watch it going up in pine two-by-sixes, an odd sight that I still see sometimes in early morning dreams — the transparent, solid future of everything I could then imagine. On the second floor we put in two fire escapes.

The house is a California Craftsman with stray Spanish influence; in other words, it is made of plain wooden boards, running vertically, with tilework around openings and, because of Elizabeth's childhood outside San Diego, an appearance from the front of being only one story. Actually it is two. The foundation is deep and the lot slopes to the rear, where by an architect's trick the second floor hides. From our bedroom we look down over the swimming pool: the water slaps and sloshes into the sidewall filters as we sleep at night, the sound not unlike that of a distant, friendly ocean.

On summer mornings the pool top swarms with maple-seed helicopters and swollen tiger bees spinning in their own odd currents. I come out every Saturday when I am not on call and clean the debris from the filter room. I unscrew the plastic cap over a week's paste of tree parts and insects clinging to the aluminum mesh. I wipe it free and set the waste in a plastic bag whose top twists with a yellow tie. At the end of two months this bag goes into a larger one in the garbage shed, from there to be picked up. There is a city not far from here that sits on such garbage.

I like to swim and try to every day. The pool is long enough for six strokes, a kickoff at each end, a breath each lap. When I come from the hospital I change into trunks, fetch Jonathan from his windowsill, and the two of us go outside, where, warm or not, I take off my shirt and we do jumping jacks together. This gets the blood flowing. Though I went to Tufts University Medical School and ought to know better, I also think the exercise brings out hair on the arms and makes a tan deeper. This is vanity, I know.

Most days Jonathan gets into the pool with me. He can swim well enough already, and does sometimes, though a five-year-old swimming laps is contrary to animal nature. He splashes at the shallow end. He floats and makes engine noises that I can hear under water on my approach. I dive under and we play at an alligator attack. I make sure to cut his nails every week for this. He thrashes and I surface, blowing streams of pool water. We wrestle until he succeeds at what I've taught him, to turn me over, and then I go limp. I float face up, looking into the evening lights and the peaceful, suburban sky. "Dead alligator," Jonathan says.

We towel off on the deck. Then we go inside, where Elizabeth and I work on dinner together in a kitchen that smells like a forest. The scent comes from the floor wax, but I am not so cynical that I cannot enjoy it, a trace of white pine while we do our chores. At my triangular corner of the counter I cut a bowlful of cucumbers and tomatoes while across the butcher block she bastes a flank steak in secret juice. Jonathan sits outside in the back yard where we can see him.

I think he does this to please us, and I am grateful for his acquiescence. He is three and a half feet tall and forty pounds. This is less than the weight of our shepherd-collie, Abraham, by a good measure. Jonathan has been going to school now for a year, and on the days I drive him, he and Abraham in the Land

Cruiser's big back seat, I often pause at stop signs and just thank God. Abraham noses the front seat if I wait too long. These are the days I am not in the operating room, and after I drop off Jonathan, I turn the car around and drive up the hill that overlooks our house. I sit up there with the engine running. I brush the seat back with my palm, and Abraham arches once and leaps into the seat next to me, where I crack the window for him. He points his snout into the morning air, his moist eyes blinking. I have a half hour to waste before I must see office patients. I sit up there with Abraham and try not to consider all the ways such a life as mine could go wrong.

This kind of worrying, the worries of a man with a wife, a child, a healthy heart, the doomsday obsessions of a straight-shouldered eye surgeon with money in three local banks — this kind of worrying has come to dominate certain times of the day. Mornings, alone, with Jonathan asleep and Elizabeth upstairs soaking her face in a particled, dermatologic gel, I walk the outside grounds and feel the rumbles of the trucks driving downhill from us on the avenue. And each time, as the lawn shakes, I think for a moment that we are having an earthquake. The leaves tremble. Who is to say I am a corrupted man, clothed in these comforts and worried so often about their loss? The sight of our roof-high poplars makes me think on some days of the majesty of God and on others of the decent possibility that in a west-blowing storm they could come down on top of the black, double-insulated electric lines of our house.

I have strayed a good bit from the places of my childhood. Then, we lived in a two-story saltbox in Blue River, Wisconsin, the fatherless three of us, on a bluff that looked out over two ochre turns of the Mississippi River. Our yard was falling little

by little into the water. From there, I suppose, it washed downhill to the Gulf of Mexico, our little bit of grass and dirt, slipping away behind us to add to the gathering, seaward reach of
Louisiana. It was an eroding cliff, our homestead, though this
idea was lost on me; it still is, except when I have two drinks
before dinner and begin to think about the causes of things. I
was essentially a happy child. There are two kinds of children,
and I was that one. Lawrence was the other.

Fifteen years ago, in Blue River, I left him off at the bus to go to
California. Since then I have heard almost nothing about him,
just little bits from our sister, Darienne, who is a music teacher
now in St. Louis; she is, in a way, all that keeps us together. Our
brother just rode away that day out of our lives. By the time I
rode away myself, three years later, to South Bend, Indiana, for
college, I'd heard from him only once, in a postcard mailed from
Bolinas, California, where he said he was working in com-
puters. By the time I got to medical school he'd left that, or so
Darienne told me, and we heard no more of him until seven or
eight years ago; he was involved in some kind of communal
business and living arrangement then. Darienne told me about
that one also. A few months later he wrote to her again, but
when she went out to visit him he wasn't at his address. Now
and then she got other letters from him, and in one he apolo-
gized for not being there when she arrived. There was no explanation, just a few words saying he was sorry. Darienne sent me
a copy of that one. It was written on a Lyon's restaurant place-
mat, his small, squarish print slanting down across the lightly
waxed back. He was dealing blackjack in a gambling casino
near the Nevada border, he wrote. When I read that in the letter

I pictured the cards fanning out flat from the flicks of his big, cheater's hands.

After breakfast we bring Lawrence to the guest room and Elizabeth finds him some clothes of mine to wear. My Notre Dame sweatshirt fits him in the chest, though his wrists stick out a good way. Elizabeth gives him a pair of my blue jeans and throws his trousers in the washer. I listen to the water churning through its cycle, the drain hose pouring dirt from his mysterious life into our downstairs utility sink.

Jonathan and I go with him into the kitchen. I put Jonathan to work peeling bologna from the sliced delicatessen block while I set out bread and make an assembly line of it. Lawrence chops lettuce. I arrange it, with tomatoes, mustard, and the sweet sandwich spread Elizabeth and Jonathan like. To me the spread tastes like sugar and nothing more, but I put it on my own anyway because for some reason it seems right to me that on a family picnic everybody should have the same sandwich. Lawrence keeps chopping. When I look again he has chopped the whole head of lettuce. It lies in kinked ribbons on the counter.

"We're making four sandwiches," I say. "You didn't have to chop the whole thing."

He looks hurt. With his fingers he moves the cut piles into one heap and presses them together.

"That's all right, Lawrence."

I take Jonathan's bologna, broken at the edges from his fingers, and finish the sandwiches. The top slice, pressed down, gives softly in the air-filled way of modern bread. This always pleases me. I flip them into closable bags, and at that moment I realize Jonathan has noticed my brother's hand. He stands behind the open door of the refrigerator, the half-closed bologna block on the shelf, looking up toward where Lawrence moves it amid the cut lettuce.

"Lawrence," I say, "what have you been doing all these years?"

"I'm living in Nevada," he says. "I have a place there. I'm working casino."

"You're dealing cards?"

"No, I stopped."

He begins playing with the lettuce again, moving his hand around the chopped leaves. "Close the refrigerator," I say to Jonathan, "and go get your mother."

He runs out of the room, and I turn back to Lawrence. "Why'd you stop dealing?"

"People weren't coming to my table."

"Why not?"

"They don't like cripples."

I make a stack of the four sandwiches. "In the eyes of God," I say, "we're all cripples."

"What?"

"It's what Mom used to say."

He comes around the butcher block. Its surface, maple coated with mineral oil, shines waxily, and across it he lays his left arm. "What are the two bones, Ed?"

"Come on, Lawrence."

"What are they?"

"Radius and ulna."

"Great," he says. "Bingo." He nods and straightens, a quick little dance. "On the money," he says. "You named it." He turns his wrists in the air. "The question is, would you come to my table, Ed?"

"Lawrence."

"Would you?"

"Of course I would."

At the top of the stairs Elizabeth holds Jonathan's hand. They start down but I motion out the door for them to stop, and they go back up. Leaning against the counter, Lawrence smiles. "I know you would," he says. "You think you're a decent guy." He stands up and leans against the wall. "But you're not a cripple, Edward. *I'm* a cripple. You're an ophthalmologist with a pool." He points out the kitchen window to where the black solar tarp lies covering it. "And I don't give a damn about the eyes of God."

Our lives are good. I know it, and although I am tempted to apologize for this as well, I will not. For a time during my internship I considered leaving my profession: I brooded and tried to keep my patients out of the hospital. I told them they probably didn't need to stay, that their conditions were less serious than we imagined and their belly pain was probably gas; for the most part, I knew, it was. After surgery, when they settled in for a week of hospital meals and three-hour nurse checks, I told them they could go home in two days. Some of them laughed. This strained their suture lines, but I told them I was serious: we kept them here because that's how we got paid. I was getting nowhere with my point, however. I told a couple of other surgeons about it, and they nodded, practicing their deep-hole knots as I talked.

I could have become fiery. At night I sat in the doctors' lounge, and when the other surgeons came in I stepped out onto the balcony overlooking the ocean. Shore birds there flew back and forth; through the open windows I heard the IV pumps clicking on and off. In Africa, whole villages went blind from the bites of stream flies: these were the thoughts I had; in India, burned corpses drifted on the Ganges. Mankind, for those weeks, seemed more devilish to me than any imagined devil, and as a foolish consequence I stood on that balcony and considered leaving medicine. It seemed to me that a decent man ought to devote himself to good works, and this was the kind of man I believed I was. Seagulls landed at my feet.

In my free hours, which were few, I wandered outside the hospital. In those days the neighborhood was called transitional, and each time I left the front hall the guard offered to call me a cab. I walked at night in my light blue surgical scrubs and the pillow-sized foot covers we wore for cleanliness. Nobody bothered me. Since then, I have heard of razor slashings and small gunfights in that neighborhood, but I had about me then the shield of conviction. I walked, angry and righteous.

In the long run, however, what was I supposed to do? The world offered me a wife, a child, a house: that the house had two thirds of a gardened acre around it, that the child's school taught Greek and Latin — are these things I should have spurned? For a few months during the balmy middle of that year, my conscience burned. Since then, though, that burning has passed, faded into the eucalyptus-scented afternoon air. Now, in the downstairs of our Spanish-Craftsman house where the refrigerator has two doors and makes its own ice, where the front yard floodlights sense evening with their own circuits, my thoughts include whether to add more chlorine to the pool because my brother's clothes smell as though he may have been in it.

In the kitchen now with the sandwiches set inside the little plastic bags, my brother walks over, stands by the sink, and does something he knows I will not like. The sink's aluminum skirt, washed and sponged daily, gleams dully in light from the yard. On the windowsill sit two small clay flower pots, their African violets drooping in the warmth; next to one is a water glass that holds barber's shears, an indelible black marker, a tangle of paper clips, and two boxes of matches. Lawrence fingers a box, then turns on the faucet. It chokes once — the washer with his clothes is still on — then spits out its air-whitened stream. He moves the handle back and forth, watching the sphere of the aluminum ball and socket, then the spiral of water down the inclined sink bed into the drain.

The matches are from Jatte Française, a steak house near here, and stamped on the cover is a French flag, three colors. They are thick-stemmed and easy to light, a ball of blue-green sulfur at the tip: he opens them. Standing over the counter, he takes one out and strikes it. He throws it into the sink while the water is still running, and as it sizzles he lights another. This one he lets burn down farther, holding it with his elbow angled up to the window. When the flame nears his thumbnail, he flicks it quickly in the air, and it drops into the sink. It hisses, or perhaps I only imagine the hiss, and I think of him years ago, standing on the bluff behind our house in Wisconsin, lighting matches from American Beauty Hardware, matches that were thin and made of laminated paper and nestled in books with a silver rose, one color, stamped on the cover. He used to light them and watch them fall into the Mississippi. I stood next to him. We were brothers then. They extinguished in the drop, but halfway down, where the river wind swirled, they sometimes took flight and climbed, reaching us at the top of the cliff, where the thin trails of smoke disappeared while we waited and watched, hoping for the rare match that burst to flame again before our eyes.

In the kitchen now he takes out another one. "The zoo gets crowded after noon," I say.

"Ah," he says. "Then let's go."

Life, I know, had given to me what it has not given to many others: a sense of importance in my work, and rightness, and security in the wood-and-tile house I own and insure; the wall-to-wall, thick-pile, stain-resistant carpet there transmits to me, I sometimes think, the same warmth and ease of breath that a caveman must have felt in the skin of a bison or a musk ox. I suspect that for a woman this feeling is not the same; for I do believe that, despite what is often said, women are in some way less afraid than men and therefore less in need of this kind of comfort. Elizabeth likes the wooden floors of the downstairs, for example, and does not understand why I like to take off my shoes and stand barefoot on the carpet. Late at night, when she and Jonathan are asleep, I stand shoeless at the head of the stairs and look through the small window on the landing, out into the mostly dark neighborhood and beyond it to the lighted Mormon church in the hills. It stands there among the swaying cypresses like a glowing, alabaster rocket. Around me our house creaks as though alive. These are the creaks of studs and headers and sill plates, the shimmying of nails in the California air that is dry all night until dawn brings in fog from the sea. I know this, but it still seems like a gesture to me, a nod from our house when the rest of the family sleeps and only I am there to hear it. I pat the wall.

What I also do sometimes is this: I leave the landing, put my shoes back on, and go out to the garage, where Abraham wakes devotedly and hops into the Land Cruiser with me, and together we drive down the hills out to the freeway. This is in the dead of night and except for the rarest car heading down the hill beside us, we are dead alone. These drivers, I like to imagine, are fishermen or bakers, although I know they are more likely stock traders awake for the market's opening in the East. One or two will wave at us, although we cannot see each other's faces. What used to puzzle me was the noise of our garage door opening, that the bump and chain-coil of its slide did not wake Elizabeth. Our bedroom is right above the garage, and though my wife is a heavy sleeper I am convinced that she is aware of what I do yet chooses not to say so. Where could she imagine I am going? Does she think I have a lover? Of course I do not.

But perhaps what I do is worse. At the freeway Abraham and I head south, because this is away from the city and deeper into the part of the country where the lots have not yet been divided; now and then along the road one still sees a stable. The freeway is eight lanes wide. Three or four cars are usually in view, and in the mirror I will sometimes see another. To the west, fog rests on the hilltops but does not yet spill down into the valley; to the east, the reservoir is blacker than the night. This highway, a sign says, has been judged by someone to be the most beautiful in the country, and driving it I can certainly see why — especially by day when the hills are gold and the live oaks stand alone in them like statues. But here at night, what I see is the shining wetness of the asphalt and the gently curving line of reflectors, set regularly into the divider stripes as they bank and fall away into the curves. This to me is also beautiful, though I would not say so to anyone. The loveliness of this road is a secret of the engineers and me, how the curves tilt gently and the damp asphalt is such new black that at certain angles it turns white in my headlights. I know these curves perfectly, and they are everywhere: nowhere here is there a flat-out stretch. The headlights shine back at me with this mysterious color change of jewels, and sometimes, although certainly not always, and though I cannot say what makes me choose the times I do, I close my eyes.

I keep them closed. I know these curves so well that I can guide the car perfectly, banking so that at times it seems we are in an airplane. I am so delicately balanced and aware of the tilted roadbed that my arms compensate for the tap of the dog's paws on the seat next to me. For half a minute at a stretch I dare myself not to look, following the gentle curves I know by memory, counting down from thirty, told of my slight errors only rarely, by the chatter of reflector bumps on tires: still with my eyes closed, I drift the car the other way. I do this once or twice a month. The road is nearly empty and the chance is small I will ever come across another car; but still, the risk is senseless, and one that flies against the basis of my life and work. I wonder why I do it. In medicine there are gambles too, but every one is well considered and embarked upon with the aim of an exact miracle. Here instead there is no purpose. With my eyes closed I sometimes imagine the hidden obstacle — a man, a car, a fallen tree — and yet I drive on, down the curves, the car held true more by these engineers' calculations than by my arms, yet held there nonetheless while we fall together blindly, Abraham and I, along a calculated curve and bank, away into the night.

I have always been made silent by zoos and museums, and at the city aquarium can watch the electric eels, as still as assassins, for half the afternoon. I used to do this during my residency. The streetcar took me to the city aquarium, where I walked upstairs, zealous and alone, still in my blue scrubs from the hospital. I picked one tank each visit and stood in front of it. Approaching an animal so close was a suspension of nature's wary side, and a small miracle not unlike the miracle of anaesthesia. I felt the same forbidden tingle standing a hand's length from a circling hammerhead shark as I did when the scalpels I wielded made their first painless cuts into an abdomen. For a moment God and nature looked the other way.

It is late morning before we pack the Land Cruiser and set off, the four of us, for the zoo. I drive. Elizabeth sits in back with Jonathan. On the baggage deck Abraham paces left and right, his nose leaving prints on the windows. Next to me Lawrence leans forward, staring through the windshield. I take a long route, cutting back to avoid our neighborhood. I'm grateful for Lawrence's poor directional sense, yet each time we pass a swimming pool or a row of head-high cypress hedges, he makes a low whistling sound. I make a wrong turn and we pass a Spanish stucco, tile-roofed mansion with a gate two stories tall, and he says, "Look at that, Jonathan. A castle."

Jonathan sits back in the seat. His shyness has returned and he keeps his gaze outside the car. I'm grateful for this, though puzzled at a five-year-old's being embarrassed — for this, it seems to me, is what he is. But what does he have to be embarrassed about, even if it's another person's misfortune? He is silent.

"For a moment, I thought we were already at the zoo," says Lawrence.

In the mirror I see Jonathan blink twice, then turn to the window again. Lawrence makes a monkey sound, and I drive down more back streets.

"What are you doing in the casino, then?"

We drive another block. "Security systems," he answers.

"What does that mean?" asks Elizabeth.

"Those places need security," I say to her. In the mirror I am looking into her egg-shaped eyes. "You'd be amazed at the problems they have. Professional gamblers come into the places in disguise. Not to mention other problems."

"I'm a guard," says Lawrence.

"Do you have a gun?" asks Jonathan.

"Jonathan!" says my wife.

"Jonathan, Lawrence is a security guard. He's not a policeman."

"Yeah, I have one," says Lawrence.

"You do not."

"Listen, Ed."

"What should we do first at the zoo?" says Elizabeth.

"You better not have it here," I say.

"Let's see the monkeys," says Lawrence.

"Monkeys," says Jonathan.

"I'm serious, Lawrence."

Everybody stops talking. In the mirror Jonathan's face has reddened and he holds it stiffly, his eyes not blinking, toward the glass. Lawrence begins whistling. He puts his left hand on the dashboard, on top, near my defroster vent.

"Okay," he says.

"Okay what."

"Okay, let's talk about the zoo." He rolls down his window and sticks his head out into the wind. He grits his teeth. Abraham starts to bark. "I love the monkeys," he shouts ahead of us, and Jonathan laughs for the second time today.

In Jonathan's class at school there is a bigger boy, already square in his face, who stares at everybody. He has been kept back a grade, though I understand from Elizabeth that his aptitude is high. When I first met him he looked at me fiercely, his black eyes unblinking, his body still. This was at the schoolyard where I waited one afternoon for Jonathan. What was it he wanted? I thought to myself. His father owns the small grocery where we buy late night milk; his mother lives in another town. In his unbroken, puff-lidded gaze I saw the look of the man who leans over the register at midnight to put a carton in my bag. The father, I had heard, beat him.

The boy's name is Jesse. For some reason he is the schoolmate Jonathan has chosen to befriend, though Jesse is six inches taller and half again as heavy; he walks fast, his cheeks pursed up so that his eyes are half closed; he throws rocks, in a hard and determined way, across the schoolyard and across the street; he laughs accusingly. At the playground I have seen him standing at the middle of a group of boys in his torn shirt. As if anger could cause a child to grow faster, as if it lived not only in his house above the grocery but in his blood and muscle too, he looks several years older than the rest of them. I half-expect to see hair on his upper lip. Now and then Jonathan wears a torn shirt, too. It is yellow cotton and ripped at the seam where the sleeve reaches the shoulder.

Jesse came to our house once. Jonathan wanted him over, and, although the boy bothered me, I went to the grocery to pick him up. It was a recent Saturday, the air was hot, and inside the store the coolers hummed, spreading clouds of frost on the glass cases. A man in sandals and jeans bought a carton of cigarettes and played a lottery ticket, while Jesse's father, dark and sullen, stood behind the register watching a small TV. I looked at the boxes of cottage cheese in the dairy case until the other man made his purchases, and then I went to the counter with a carton of milk. He rang it up, took my money, slipped it with one motion into the white bag, handed it across the counter, and turned back to the program. "You come to get Jesse?" he finally said, not looking at me.

"Yes, I did, if that's all right with you."

"What would anybody want with Jesse?" He reached across and changed the channel.

"My son Jonathan is friends with him at school."

"Friends with him at school." He still hadn't looked at me. "I still don't see what anybody would want with him."

I put my elbow on the counter and pretended to watch the television. What could I have said to him? On top of his head he was bald and had combed over hair from the other side. I smelled his lime aftershave. When he turned from the set and looked at me, the dark irises were blank.

Jesse came down then, opening a door at the back of the store and stepping into the short aisle. In the unnatural darkness where he stood — the windows there were taped with brown plastic — he looked ill at ease and puny. His hair was greasy, standing up where he had combed it, and his sneakers were untied. He didn't look at me either, just shuffled down the aisle and stood several feet from us, squinting out the one untaped window bottom to the brilliant day on the sidewalk. He ran his fingers through his hair.

"This man here's the other boy's father," said the grocer.

"Hello, Jesse. I'm here to pick you up."

"Can't see why, though," said the grocer.

That afternoon, they played in our back yard and in Jonathan's room and in the long, carpeted hallway of our basement. Jesse was stronger than Jonathan. He ran faster, his trousers tight around his plump legs. That didn't bother me. Inside, with Elizabeth, I considered bringing up what I was afraid of — the fierce stares I had seen in the schoolyard, the same dark irises in the grocery store. I considered bringing it up, but I didn't. They were playing more or less equally, Jonathan running two steps behind, hesitating a moment before jumping from the hedge landing; Jesse leaping ahead, bouncing, landing, his arms and legs thrown forward. But that was all right; in school Jonathan would outstrip Jesse one day, and I thought it better for the moment that he learn trepidation. I thought he should learn to follow, to take confidence in his own fears and use them as a guide. He ran without bending his thin arms. He jumped leaning slightly backward, fear weighting his flight, and landed with a quick hop to the rear. Jesse sped, in and out of bushes and chairs, around the thick-trunked juniper. He yelled. His shouts — Indian shouts, robber shouts, hoots — rose to where Elizabeth and I sat upstairs in the sun room; Jonathan, his voice soft in a way I hoped would later mean kindness, shouted after him.

Elizabeth and I were reading. We listened to the yard sounds made by the two of them, to the shouts and footfalls and the obese squash of our underinflated rubber ball. They ran, then sat, then ran again. We read. As a child, I too had been quiet. Not shy, exactly, but without the fierceness Lawrence made use of. He did what he wanted: he cut wild, wandering paths in the world; I, years later, made my easier way through a wilderness already half settled. He fought. In parking lots and fields, behind houses and later behind liquor stores, he launched his fists at the world. He shouted and swung chains. He came home bleeding. I, in my whole life, have only once swung my fist.

That afternoon, when the air had just begun to cool, we heard them go into the pool. Jonathan knew how to swim from the time we spent together, but I was worried about Jesse. Looking out the window I saw him, but he surprised me: he was remarkably able in the water, floating on his back and his side, diving under with legs straight and calves together, his red ankles pointing into the five o'clock sky. As I watched, he surfaced. Then he dove again, circling around Jonathan, the blue-black shark's shape of his body broken by the refraction of the surface. Jonathan squealed. Jesse surfaced behind him, splashing. The water flew. Jonathan turned, firing back, his small hands beating the water. The two boys splashed, triangles of aquamarine turning colorless in the air, shouting, beating each other back, ducking under the chopped blue to flee. Jesse's arms, bigger, threw sheets of water. Jonathan aimed and darted. I went back to reading.

When I looked out again, a time later, I saw this: Jesse leaning back neck-deep against the concrete side wall, while Jonathan, my own boy, approached him, swimming half-submerged, his thin arms breaking the water from fatigue. Jonathan approached him again and again, and Jesse reached out each time and easily dunked him, held him down while Jonathan's arm, his hand, his small shoulder, struggled to the surface; once, Jesse held him down so long I stepped out onto the balcony. Then he released him. Jonathan, gasping, threw back his head in the evening light and breathed air — once, twice, then crossed the pool again and made his weak attack. Jesse, standing, reached across and dunked him again. I was going to say something but didn't. He held Jonathan down. Twisting from the shoulder, gripping the small crown of my son's head two feet under, he grimaced, pumped up and down, so long again that I felt words rising in my throat; then he released him. And Jonathan again crossed the pool to catch his breath; he paused at the wall and then returned.

What was he doing, swimming, reswimming those fifteen feet of choppy surface to be pushed under it one more time? He didn't know about the world, that it turned all the way around. I wanted to shout to him from the balcony. In time, I wanted to say, he would grow beyond the thick, dunking arms of the other boy. His weakness, the pale, thin draw of his chest — these were not things to be punished. But he thought they were. The trouble, the strife of the grocer and his wife, now dark-armed and half-floating in our pool, drew him. He swam. Back and again he returned to collect his punishment. As I once did, he ran toward cruelty.

Once, for a few weeks, I saw a psychiatrist about this habit of mine. I did so discreetly, of course, as a man in my position must, for who would trust his sight to a doctor with such an urge? In a facile way I pointed out to him that driving with my eyes closed on a wide nighttime highway pre-empted any foolish risk I might take in an operating suite, and though at this explanation he nodded forcefully and blinked down into his beard, I knew, in the quiet way I have always known things in my life, that this was not exactly true.

His name was Dr. Belfast and his office was upstairs in a house. From the sidewalk in his neighborhood one would never have guessed a man worked here in the business of the mind. The fences were painted and the hedges clipped into shapes. I would park two blocks away, around the corner, and take Abraham on his braided leash for cover. I arrived early for every session and we walked up a hill, down a hill, and around the corner onto the gently sloping sidewalk that ran by his house, dappled in the uneven shade of California oaks and cypresses. We entered through the side alley.

He let Abraham sit with me for our visits, although I was aware that my bringing a dog meant as much to a man of his profession as the bulge of veins on a retina might have meant to a man in mine. Abraham rested his snout across his paws. Dr. Belfast would turn in his chair and fold his arms. I would sit, look momentarily into the black tangle of his beard, and begin. It was only this we talked about, my driving, because it was only this, to my own thinking, that lacked an explanation in the seduction of my life; everything else that I wanted and feared had roots in the warm air, the soft carpet, the gentle touch of this land and house and family that, like a miracle, had come to me unbidden. Dr. Belfast did not believe this. He wanted further explanations; he wanted to talk about Elizabeth, my mother, Jonathan, Lawrence, about the fears I have at night when the bustle of the neighborhood grows still and the sounds of airplanes and creaking houses can be heard; he wanted to talk about love and shelter and this work I do, touching pinpoint knives to blue and brown and hazel irises, to the single circle of beauty in the miraculous geometry of the eye. But I did not talk of this with him; I kept the conversation to my single, inexplicable habit, which seemed in those days to come about as often as did these visits themselves; I did this partly because I had been trained in a surgeon's practicality, and partly because, although I would not have said this, I believe that most of a life should never be explained.

Dr. Belfast would nod.

"I have done it again," I'd say.

"Tell me."

I would nod myself, and then, as was our custom, tell him what I was thinking as I slipped the car blindly away down the incline, around the long curve abutting the reservoir, and back up the shallow hill whose rise and summit I could sense in my knees and legs and the hollow feeling back of my skull. He had a theory, as most in his profession do, that it was a question of control, but I liked him anyway, I admit, because the first time he told me this he nodded with his lids turned down, the posture of a man without conviction, as though to say to both of us that what he had just professed contained in fact no more than a shadow of the truth.

While we walk at the zoo that morning, the fog thins and dries, the sun working its westward arc across the meridien. Through the clouded air it looks like the moon, bone-white and round as a nickel. I watch it. Elizabeth walks behind, dropped back there because Jonathan is walking with Lawrence, and I am in the lead. We have unknowingly surrounded them. Ten feet back she ambles, noticing, as she does, the details of fine and decent things. These details are usually lost to me: the stone water fountain, carved into a clamshell from a single slab; the even-spaced, redwood flower stands, newly planted with primroses, that line the walks. In them, beneath the low veiny leaves, the ground mills with insects. She stops to inspect. "*Calopteron terminale*," she calls across the asphalt path, her hands holding apart the wide-ribbed lower leaves. Then, to please him, she says, "Jonathan, a net-wing beetle," and scratches beetlelike in the air.

Ahead of them now, by the camels' smelly den, I turn and wait. *Dromedarius egyptianus*, the plaque says, and to my left, past two flower planters and a slope of close-cut grass, is the animal, female, two-humped, and the color of a winter coat. She looks at me. The legs and neck, which seem by relation partly llama and partly giraffe, hold the overfat body forward in the cage. She stretches her leather-tipped proboscis through the bars. The eyes are a woman's eyes, long-lashed and shining as though from recent weeping. I look into them. She blinks; I blink. I move sideways to the low fence that keeps me back. The smell is of wet carpet or hay. "Hello," I say. The snout, unmoving, holds steady between the bars. It is wedged there, I see, where she has thrust it forward. She is resting her neck.

The cage, our living room in size, is empty behind her. She has no mate: I pluck a lump of grass and toss it in to her.

Behind me Lawrence has lifted Jonathan. He holds him aloft, a full bony arm's length over his head, and my son's legs are scissoring slowly in the air. This, I vaguely remember from medical school, is some primitive balance mechanism, a remnant of the airborne instincts of the lemur or the tree shrew. Lawrence twists him first left, where I see that he notices in the near distance the camel's stuck-through snout, then right, over the carp pond, then back again all the way around where behind him Jonathan can see his mother, blue-skirted and bent to examine some leaves. When he twists forward again I wave and point at the camel, but he doesn't seem to notice. "Look," I say, not loud enough for him to hear, though I had actually intended only to mouth the words, and at that moment, as I seem to hear the replay of my own too-soft voice, my brother bends his arms and throws my son into the air.

Jonathan. He is reaching: forward, sideways, kicking his five-year-old legs. In my own chest there is an implosion of lightness and my arms go out. *Catch him, Lawrence*. He has turned partway forward, a half-gainer in the foggy air above my brother's head, and behind him, through the space formed by his bent waist and down the short paved hill, I see Elizabeth, looking up now also, the three of us in a line. *Lawrence, catch him*. Jonathan is turned completely over, falling head first, and this is the end of both of our lives, of all of our lives, and then Elizabeth puts her hand over her mouth, and Jonathan is still falling, and our swimming pool and our house seem to be a great distance from where we are now and, more than that, from everything we have ever hoped for, just wood and concrete and planned hedges, and then of course Lawrence puts his arms forward and catches him.

He hangs upside down. I hear him crying. I take a breath and trot down the low hill toward them while in front of me Elizabeth comes up. "Jonathan, Jonathan," I am saying, his weeping getting louder now, and I realize only when I am upon them, and my wife is too, that he is in fact laughing.

"To the monkey cage," Lawrence says.

"Give me my son."

Lawrence looks at me, his bent nose turned down and his eyes in shadow. His cheeks and nostrils puff once, twice, and then he lifts Jonathan, who has been doing dangling sit-ups, up and over and sets him on the ground. Jonathan takes a couple of steps back, then runs forward and flings himself against my brother's hips. Elizabeth puts her hand on my arm.

"Okay," I say, "I know you were just fooling around."

"Why so jumpy, champ?"

"Ed was worried for a moment," says Elizabeth.

"You're damn right I was worried."

"About what?"

"Monkey's cage," says Jonathan.

"My son was upside down in the air," I say. "That's about what."

"Jeez, Ed," he says. He smiles halfway, showing the broken line of his top teeth, tilts his head earthward, then looks up again at me with his hands out, turned forward. The two palms, little secrets of paleness, face me. The one, creased thickly where it tapers to the damaged fingers, seems to have changed over the years, wrinkled and settled around the broad carpal faces so that at that moment it doesn't strike me as sad or crippling or symbolic of anything. He lets them drop.

"To the monkey cage," I say.

We walk. The camel, womanlike again, blinks as we pass. I want to stop there, to show Jonathan the amused intelligence of those eyes and the topheavy lean of weight. But he is looking up at the sky with one hand against Lawrence's hip for balance as he walks, and it seems to me we are in a delicate situation. I scan the path in front for holes or rocks or twists of pavement that might topple him, but there is none, just the shallow hill down to the tropical cages. His arms are out, winglike. His head is tilted up. Above us, the white sky he has recently traversed opens with cracks of blue.

At the monkey cage we stop and stand along the low iron railing, thigh-height on me but a good way up Jonathan's chest. He is still looking at the sky, despite the long cage in front of us decorated with plaster tree boughs. They are perfectly made, down to the viny ropes hanging from the ceiling and the foot-wide tropical leaves at the ends of branches. From the top corner of the cage a cataract froths floorward, raising real jungle mist, its pipe source just visible through the leaves. The cage stinks. Inside it the monkeys seem a little dwarfed, not just by the size of everything but by the movement. The wind has come up, and all the huge, man-made plants are swaying. In the corner the waterfall booms. Next to it, three or four of the dark brown humps sit crouched. They look at us. The top lips are upturned, sneerish, the eyes dark as marbles. I watch the hands, the shiny, leatherish palms and the long unopposed thumbs that I consider explaining to Jonathan but decide not to. Lawrence stands at the corner of the rail, several yards from me, not moving.

I realize I don't trust him — an obvious point but one that has always been easy for me to forget. It comes to me now as we stand here, and I wonder why he has come to visit us. In front of him the monkeys do nothing except occasionally reach sideways to touch each other. One rests its hand on another's shoulder. This is more than my brother and I have done, save for the first moments in our front hallway, and I consider walking over now to stand next to him. Before I can, he hops up over the railing and walks down to the cage.

He stands peering through the bars, making a small kissing noise. Jonathan watches. Lawrence puts his arm into the cage and makes a motion, and momentarily, from the back, the rise and outward slide of his scapula is familiar. For a moment I know everything about him, my brother, Lawrence. But then he stops moving and is unfamiliar again. I look over at Jonathan.

"Lawrence," I say. I do this partly so that I can hear a sound of my own making, partly to keep my son this side of the fence. I don't really care what my brother does.

He keeps up the kissing noise. One of the monkeys watches him from its plaster pedestal, its small square head tilted forward.

Jonathan goes up on his tiptoes. "What's he doing?"

"He's being a monkey," says Elizabeth.

Lawrence crouches, holding the bars, until he is at eye level with the creature. Then he begins to hiss, short rasps through his clenched teeth, and bounce up and down. His gangly legs drop and straighten. His neck, thrust forward, bulges with each sound, and suddenly, inside the cage, the monkeys leap onto the tree limbs and start toward him. They hoot, cross one-armed back and forth from the deep inner wall toward the bars, their lips opened to the gums. The glovelike palms flex and claw, the long tails reaching, the shoulders bumping and turning, while Lawrence bounces and hisses and chatters his teeth. They come toward him with their nostrils flared, the foul smell rising and filling the walk as they move. Lawrence laughs. He leans away from the bars, grips them, and tosses back his head, his mouth open and all the sharp angles of his face turned up to the clearing sky.

And then in an instant the monkeys are calm again. They squat, haunches doubled, licking their fur, which from motion stands up in bristly streaks. Their coats shine unevenly from the licking. The waterfall pours. Lawrence turns around and comes back up, jumps the iron fence without touching it, and in this splayed leap there he is again, my brother. I study him as we walk: he has changed. Only the foundation of his face is the same, the prominent orbits — though the eyes are smaller in them now, dark and sunken — the broad, Eskimo cheekbones and the angled nose that is faintly Inca or Cherokee. Now, watching him, I see again what I have known all my life but have forgotten: that the face, the clavicle, the whole body, is larger on the right side than on the left. Then this vision vanishes also, and we are just two men again, walking, and I cannot see him anymore.

At the carp pond we stop to rest and he lifts Jonathan onto his shoulders. It is already midafternoon, and for the rest of the day, while the air, now clear, begins to chill, we wander among the cages. Lawrence keeps Jonathan on his shoulders. We see brown bears, round-jointed and padding tenderly on their platform; we see iguanas; we see two tigers and a small herd of llamas with their amused, ocular expressions. Between cages Jonathan stays on Lawrence's shoulders. "Good horsy," he says, patting the bony blades as my brother moves through the afternoon crowd. Lawrence ducks and bobs, speeds up to sneak between passing couples, slows down abruptly and pretends to fall forward so that Jonathan squeals. He hops onto the footbridge over the duck pond. It is wooden and arched high in a Japanese way. At its middle he stops, then leans side to side, a good way over the railing, so that Elizabeth and I see their faces — his angled and dark, Jonathan's round and pale — in the still water.

Here and there goldfish rise, their lips puckering the surface and sliding under. I watch my brother and my son standing above the dirty water that is oil-smooth but for the pocks of fish ripples. Lawrence leans over again. Jonathan lets go with his hands this time and hangs upside down, his red-brown hair as straight as broom straw, nearly dipping in the water. Elizabeth touches my arm. "He's good with him, your brother," she says.

The last time I saw Lawrence was the only time in my life that I have seen our father. He left our mother two months before I was born, one warm spring, driving away in a Rambler coupe he had just bought her with money he had stolen from his company. A friend of our mother's was in the seat next to him. Lawrence was six then, Darienne was not yet three, and I was still in the womb, kicking my half-formed knees until our mother cried out. She told me the kicking started when the Rambler left.

I have no father at all to remember, and even now see him only as he stands in one of Darienne's paintings on our study wall, a painting of how she imagined the five of us would look together, leaning against the shining, rain-dropped hood of that same Rambler. We are arm in arm. Our father's hair is black and his nose is bent, the way my brother's is now. He is smiling down at us. Elizabeth says I too resemble him, although for the life of me I cannot see this.

The only time I saw him was in the VA hospital in El Paso, Texas, five years ago, where we thought he was going to die. A day earlier, Lawrence had called me from the House of Pancakes across the street from the emergency room, reversing the charges, waking us one Sunday morning at sunrise. "Collect from Lawrence," said the operator, and I had to think for a moment, emerging from sleep, Elizabeth leaning up next to me in her soap-smelling nightgown, of who by that name could be calling me. "He's there to die," Lawrence whispered.

A day later in El Paso we walked to the hospital together, Lawrence striding ahead of me, turning around to tell me what he knew of our father's life. My brother looked reasonably well then: his shirt was pressed. The air was bright with southern sun and filled with dust. The old man had been living in the Southwest, Lawrence said — first New Mexico, then Arizona, now Texas — working as an engineer for the fuel companies. He'd done well — two cars and a swimming pool. We walked on toward the hospital. The woman who had driven off in the Rambler with him — our mother's friend — wasn't with him anymore. Lawrence looked at me when he said that, turned around on the sidewalk and walked backward, peered at me with his head tilted forward. He'd married someone else, though: he had a wife but no new children. We were at the hospital by then. And even though he had a new wife, he had a new girlfriend, too, and she was in the room with him. Lawrence told me this and we went in.

How can I describe what I saw in that three-bed, government-sponsored recovery room, decorated with paper flowers and crinkled bunting from the ladies' auxiliary, two spots taken up by bloat-skinned strangers and the third by a man I guessed was our father only because Lawrence bowed slightly and cleared his throat and stepped toward that bed? In it an old man turned and looked at me. He was bloat-skinned also, like the other fellows, and his face had the yellowish cast — the almost powdered look — that by then I knew well enough meant kidney disease. This man was my father. A young woman — in her late forties, I would guess — leaned forward from the far side of the bed, touched her breast, and stood. "Oh, my," she said. "You must be Edward." She came around the bed and hugged me. There were so many hospital smells I hated in that room — iodine, sheet soap, waffle syrup from the plastic breakfast trays — that her lemon hairspray thrilled me the way forest air or an ocean surf might have. The sight of my father made me uneasy — it repulsed me, really — and at that moment, though it humiliates me now to think of it, I was so grateful for the hard, blond set of his mistress's hairdo and the sweet scent of her perfume that I hugged her as tightly as I would my own mother. Our father, the old powdery man in the bed, rumpled his nostrils.

"So —" I said to him.

He waved his hand to silence me, the thin palm hanging from the wrist and covered in its own yellowish frost. His mistress stepped back and eyed me familiarly.

"Ed," said my father, "it pleases me to introduce you to Natalie." He nodded toward the foot of his bed, where she stood. "Natalie," he said, "my son Edward."

"Pleased to meet you, Natalie."

"That's enough of that," said my father. "You probably want to pull the plug on me, don't you, Ed?"

"Don't be ridiculous," said Natalie.

Who's being ridiculous?

The hand moved again, made another small gesture of dismissal, though I realized now that there had been some neurologic damage. The fingers arched and brushed sideways, as though shooing an insect, and I saw underneath the pushed-back sheets that the nurses had tied him down. White cloth straps pinched his arm below the elbow and led to the aluminum side rails of the bed — posies, they were called. I saw that they had tied one foot as well, though the other was free and lay above the sheets. An IV disappeared into the skin below his clavical. This, I guessed, was the reason for the straps — that an old oil digger like him probably pulled the line out of his chest every time the surgical resident ran it in there. I'd done it myself a dozen times, strapped down the hands of the old guys so I could sleep at night. I looked at our father's face again. Little drops of lubricating ointment beaded on his top lip.

"I'm asking him if he wants to pull the plug on me, Lawrence." He lifted his head toward me, then shifted his eyes toward the power outlet by my feet. "Go ahead and kick it," he said. "You think I don't know you want to?"

"It goes to the EKG," I said. "It wouldn't hurt you."

"Edward's a surgeon," Natalie said to the nurse at the other bed.

"Say what you mean, for chrissake," said our father.

"I came here to see you. Lawrence said you were in a bit of trouble."

"I said I thought you were going to die this time," said Lawrence.

"That *I* was going to die?"

"Yup."

"Ed," said my father, "you're the doctor. Tell the old man whether he's going to die." He kicked away the sheet and lifted his free leg straight up from the hip, held it pointed at the three rows of fluorescent lights on the ceiling until the muscles began to shake. "Is that a man who's about to kick the bucket?"

"Put down the leg, sport," I said.

He lifted it higher. It dropped slightly and he yanked it up straight again, pointed his scaly foot skyward like a diver. The thick yellow nails curled over in front.

"You look good to me," I said.

"You're damn right I do." He let the leg drop.

"The doctors say he's doing very well," said Natalie.

"Quiet, angel."

"Edward," she said. "We're all so glad you could come."

"I want to talk to him," said our father.

"Lawrence asked me to come out."

"I thought he should see you," said Lawrence.

"I want to talk to him *now*."

"He's right here next to you, honey."

"I want him alone." He looked around at the three of us

standing over his bed. "I want an examination. He's the only one around here who'll tell me what's really up."

"I'd need to see the chart."

"I want an examination."

"I'm an ophthalmologist."

"So?"

"An eye doctor."

"Oh, for chrissake."

"Why don't Lawrence and I take a little walk?" said Natalie. She nodded forcefully at my brother. "Come on, Lawrence."

"Wait a minute," I said. But they didn't. She took his elbow and they were out into the hall; the big, pneumatic-hinged door swung back and clicked into place. I sat down. Our father looked at me. I looked back at him. Across from us, behind the half-drawn curtain and beyond the other two beds, the window was darkening. I figured the nurses would be bringing dinner soon. I cleared my throat. He kept looking at me. His sclera were yellowish and dull, enough so that I figured his liver wasn't working very well either. I cleared my throat again. "I have a brand-new son," I said.

He didn't say anything.

"You're a grandfather."

"Look," he said, "let's not kid around."

"I'm not kidding around."

"I want to get a couple of things straight." He tried to turn sideways, but his arms were held by the restraints, and he had to lie back down. The covers fell off him. I leaned forward and put them back.

He worked his nostrils, trying to loosen the tape where the oxygen lines went in. "You weren't even born yet, you know. Lawrence was older. He should be the one who's mad, right?" He worked his lips. "But you're the one, not him."

"I wouldn't have even recognized you. I came because Lawrence asked me. I've never seen you before."

He eyed me. "Your mother put that in you."

"Put what in me?"

"What you just said. She put that bitterness in you."

I looked out the window at an airplane. "So," I said, "how are you feeling?"

He cleared his throat, leaned sideways, and spit a little ball of phlegm into the kidney-shaped container hanging from the rail. Then he flopped back. "Hey," he said, "come here."

"I'm here."

"No, closer. Come down here so I can say something to you."

I looked at him. He had hair in his ears, on his neck, and in his nose. I leaned toward that nose, toward the gummy, fishlike mouth without teeth, toward the peppermint smell of his cologne. His skin was waxy. When I was close to him, he winked. "Listen," he whispered. "Why don't you just off the old bugger?"

I glanced at my watch.

"Kill me," he said. "It's what you ought to want to do. I already asked Lawrence to, but he won't. He's not brave enough." He breathed deeply through his taped nostrils. "While they're all out in the hall there. Go ahead."

"I'm going to go get them."

"No, wait." He gestured with his hand again, slinging it sideways in the restraints. "Don't do that." He smiled. "I got to ask you to do something else first."

"What is it?"

I stood and he looked up at me, smiling a salesman's grin, without teeth, his yellow eyes rolled back and his mouth pulled sideways so that I saw into the caverns of his cheeks. He lifted his hands against the cloth ties. "If you're not going to kill me, then let me out of here. Get these things off me."

"Is that what you were going to ask?"

"We're both human beings."

"I can't."

"The hell you can't." He slapped his wrists against the straps and shook his tied leg.

"Take it easy."

"I'm a prisoner in here. If you take these things off I'll go right through the window there, and that's that."

"You're no spring chicken."

"I know there's a porch out there. I'll go right out to the car and that's the last you'll ever see me." He lowered his voice. "Now, take these things off."

I checked my watch again. "What made you leave us?" I asked.

"Don't start with that. Get me out of here."

"It doesn't matter. I'm just curious."

He stopped shaking. "Jesus Christ," he said. "You're just like your mother. I'll tell you this. One day you're going to know what made me leave you. One day in your doctor's office or out at the pool you'll figure it out."

He lay back, yellow-eyed and stinking of peppermint. He was suddenly calm. We were in Texas, a place I'd never been before, and this was the last time I was ever going to see him. "Bastard," he said, jerking his hand at me, and turned his face toward the window. "Coward. Just like your brother."

This evening, after we have returned from the zoo and while Lawrence is upstairs napping in the guest room, I take a walk with Jonathan and Abraham. I like the nearby neighborhoods, the hedged and fenced ones a half mile to the west. They are as privileged as our own but neater, with square bushes and bright lawns that run to the sidewalk as clipped as mustaches. I like to walk among such calm, though I suspect that something there has gone foul in the spirit and in the mind. What is it about the children here that they seem not to have learned the lesson of right and wrong? I see them that night, limp-haired and with sullen stares they have borrowed from their parents, who are at that moment probably lounging in their back yards, holding vodka tonics in twelve-ounce tumblers etched with sailboats, wondering where their kids have gone. These kids look at us as we pass. They look at us from the front yards, from the front steps, from the front bumpers of their fathers' cars, stretched tight with black vinyl mudguards. They wear high-topped sneakers, untied. When I nod they do not smile, and — more than that — they do not look away. Abraham's clipped paws tap the sidewalk.

As usual, I am worrying. Jonathan walks behind me, letting his feet slap heel to ball, now and then pulling Abraham by his braided leash in a way that shows me the cruelty he may one day be capable of. Abraham, wise and old by dog years, follows, his wet snout touching and lifting from the hedges. At curbs Jonathan gives a sharp yank on the leash and Abraham jerks up, his heavy-lidded eyes knowing: this is a child, Jonathan is finding the first things in the world he can master. Prophetlike, the dog goes along. We cross the street. My son, told each bedtime by his mother to check and check again for traffic at corners, now takes on this mysterious chore of civilization. "Now look both ways, Abey," he says sharply, and even the inflection is his mother's, softened and turned up at the end so that the statement, like most of Elizabeth's, is at once both command and question. Abraham hops two-pawed onto the asphalt. Jonathan, all shoulder and hip, pulls back on the leash for tension, checks south and north for traffic, and then follows, his skipping gait both happiness and consternation that this four-pawed beast is ahead of him now, his maned neck thrust forward so that controlled and controller have switched in the crosswalk. Both of them hop the far-side gutter. Then we are up, ambling again among the bright green lawns.

"What do you make of these kids, Captain?" I ask him as we pass two of them on a stoop.

"Scary."

"Why scary?"

"Don't know," he says, his feet flopping again. He looks down. Strangely, this is what he always does when he has told the truth. After a fib, on the other hand, he looks us blankly in the eye. This reaction puts him squarely in the group of people I like, adults who are embarrassed by the unadorned answers that come out while looking at shoetips or light fixtures or the gray-blue drizzle outside living room windows. I pat his head.

"You're right," I say, "they *are* scary." How he knows this is a mystery to me.

We walk on. At the corner a tall old man, sixty at least, in ripped blue jeans, is hauling out a garbage pail.

"How long is my uncle staying?" Jonathan asks.

"How long is Lawrence staying?" I consider a moment. "Jonathan," I say, "I don't know."

His blue-green irises snap up to meet mine. They stare, their frank lids unblinking. How does he know this? What small turn of voice and gesture do children sense? How does he know I am lying?

By profession I am a man of science, but I must say that intuition has always played a more than passing role in my affairs: not blind guessing, for I am the kind of man who scoffs at that, but a force of conviction that I know involves logic, though I cannot say exactly how. It is more than feeling and less than reason, and, as though it had a place within the brain, I feel it in the front and upper part of mine. It is, I think, an accumulation of detail, a hidden conglomeration of thought, a sense when things are right. Over the years I have learned to trust it. During surgery it often leads me along a particular cut across the pink underside of the lid, a saline territory in miniature, where the tiniest knives and probes seem gigantic and frightening in my hands. A man's sight depends on me. Pure reason would be incapacitating here, and it is then that intuition counts — a rabbit's foot of sorts: tiny sutures lie flat for me and hold like little dams against the blood. It is instinct, though bred in reason.

When I asked Elizabeth to marry me, I knew only with this intuition that I was right. When I thought about the prospect of all those years together, my reason urged me to restraint, but I knew by then which force I was to trust. Perhaps I was afraid myself of leaving in a Rambler. But so far our marriage has been a lucky choice, and an ease has grown between us that is to me the world's rarest blessing. This ease, in fact, is exactly what I think love is — not an excited burden, as it is often made to be, but the rarest quiet, this calm in which the restless heart can at last lie down and sleep.

But it is, for other reasons, important that I say this: that I have made essential decisions in my life based not on the facts at hand but on a feeling.

For dinner that night we cook marinated chicken at home, partly because Jonathan has become edgy from the excitement and partly because I know that the rosemary smell of the sauce Elizabeth cooks makes the house domestic, reminiscent of many things, and, I admit, enviable. Lawrence stands in the corner of the kitchen with his hands in his pockets.

I am at the sink, breaking romaine lettuce at the spine, washing it, and spinning it dry. The stalks snap and bleed their water. Elizabeth, basting at intervals, leans straight-backed over the open oven door, exciting me in her capable way. She snaps the door shut, and warm wind flows over us. I glance at Lawrence.

His eyes, cast partway down, are half covered with drooping lids. This was the way he used to look, twenty years ago: leaning slope-shouldered against the pinstriped hood of his Chevrolet; standing in the sunlit doorway of Barbara's Creamery while the entry bell rang on its metal chain; loitering on the public beach, smiling and nodding at the passing women, even the mothers with their strollers. Now, leaning lightly against the fold-out ironing board in our kitchen, Lawrence is watching the black-stockinged legs of my wife.

He looks up and sees me. His grin breaks and diminishes, then breaks again, broad-toothed. I bury a center knot of romaine in the faucet's stream and say this to myself: that he is only trying to bridge distances. Elizabeth fills the oversize syringe with chicken juice and bends down again over the open oven. I don't want to look at Lawrence because I fear I know what he is going to do, so I concentrate on the lettuce stalks, which are pale green and tightly bound to each other, shoots, really, and not yet leaves. But I can't keep looking into the sink, so I glance up and he does it: he winks.

His eyes are sideways and downcast, pointed toward Elizabeth. What am I supposed to do? She is wearing a dark corduroy skirt over the black stockings. Lawrence winks again: Are you with *me* or with *her*? And then for a moment I wonder, which am I? Are we just two men, no closer than golfing acquaintances, united in the comradely ways all men think they are united, by wariness and lust and a hope for female love that, satisfied or not, eventually turns to resignation? Or are we loyal, like brothers? In my college sweatshirt and my just-bought blue jeans, he leans against my doorjamb and, with lids half shut, eyes the legs of my wife. Jonathan, upstairs, is making his gentle squeaks on the floor joists. I don't know what to think.

"Well, you two boys must be ready to eat," says Elizabeth.

"We are, ma'am," says Lawrence softly. At this, his gentleman's voice, my wife turns full around to him. He lets just the beginning of a smile appear and then looks at his shoes, leather boat soles that are mine also. Elizabeth smiles.

"Did you call me 'ma'am'?"

"Yes, I did."

"That's not the funny way you learned to talk in Las Vegas, is it?" She puts one hand on her hip and tastes a fork's coating of chicken marinade with the other.

"Reno, ma'am," he says softly.

"Wherever it is you deal."

"Guard," I say. "Lawrence is a guard now."

He doesn't look up. "I appreciate your making supper for me," he says.

"Honey," says Elizabeth, "why don't you get Jonathan down for dinner?"

For a moment I don't want to go up there, though I don't know whether this is because I hesitate to bring my son down here where the room contains uncharted disturbances and my own flagging attempts at true convictions, or because I just don't want to leave my brother alone with my wife. Lawrence has folded his arms across his chest. Elizabeth stands across from him with the chicken. The cooling oven clicks a few times, and the chrome-and-white door, a fraction loose on its hinges, slams shut. I cry out.

"Jeez," says Lawrence.

"Sorry, everybody."

Upstairs the squeaks have stopped, and I imagine Jonathan holding still to listen. What must he be thinking? Then it occurs to me with the force of truth that I have made too much of this situation, that Lawrence is in fact shy and trying hard, that he smiles at women because for the life of him he cannot think of what to say to them. I pass him on the way out and shadow-box his shoulder.

Upstairs, Jonathan is standing silently when I enter. I have surprised him somehow. His face is upturned and open-mouthed, as close to guilty as a five-year-old can produce. I wait with my hand on the doorknob. I look around: the TV is off, his chest of blocks is closed, the walls are clean. He is wearing his pajama suit with sewn toes. With a little start, I realize that it is not guilt but embarrassment again that he is feeling, although this time it is embarrassment at me, his father, the man downstairs who was shouting. He pulls the pajamas up around his waist.

"Did I surprise you?" I ask. This is how I have seen our friends raising their children. They ask questions no adult except a dull-witted one would answer truthfully. I fully expect a denial and quick recovery. What could I be thinking?

"Are you fighting?" he says.

"Don't be silly. I came up to get you for supper. We're all waiting downstairs for you."

"Coming," he says, and slides across the oak floor on those sewn feet. He puts his hands out and I hoist him onto my back, where he pauses, then scrambles up onto my shoulders, no different in feel and weight from a medium-sized animal. Around here that would be a raccoon or, on a chilly spring morning, a skunk.

"Giddyap," he says when I duck through the door and head downstairs. He squeezes his legs tight and I pretend to gasp and lose oxygen, begin to sink to the white-carpeted stairs, down on one knee, before he giggles and lets his legs loose again. I rise, and like that we enter the kitchen, where Lawrence is standing in the corner and Elizabeth is next to him, holding open his eye and peering into it.

"There's something in it," says my brother.

"Blink."

"He tried, honey."

"Hold the top lid over the bottom one."

"He tried that too."

I lean backward, and Jonathan slides down onto the linoleum floor. "Poor Uncle Lawrence," he says.

"Oh," says my brother, blinking and stepping back, "it's out." He rubs his eye and regards the three of us, furrowing his eyebrows at Jonathan. "Why, who's that?" he says.

Jonathan squeals. I grab him again and hoist him all the way up onto my shoulders before I even think what I've done, and then Lawrence is nodding at us and feinting with his forearms and saying, "Elizabeth, I think they want to have a chicken fight."

"Chicken fight!" shouts Jonathan.

"I'll get on your shoulders," Lawrence says to my wife.

"Chicken fight!" says Jonathan again.

"Chicken dinner," says my wife. And God bless her, that statement, like a little miracle, retrieves my love for her. I set Jonathan down, and in a moment we've all gone into the dining

room, where the table is set and the two candles are already
burning.

After dinner that night when Jonathan has gone upstairs to bed,
Lawrence and I stand outside on the pool deck, our hands in our
pockets, listening to the minuscule slosh of the filter and the
laughter of a television next door. The air smells of blooms. I
slip my feet out of their sandals and begin stepping slowly
around the pool's perimeter, enjoying the cool bumpiness of
the composition surface. I am waiting for Jonathan's light to go
out. Upstairs, it burns, and through his window I see Elizabeth
lean over his bed. One more time I walk around. Steam is coming off the water.

Above us, Jonathan's room is now dark. I circle the pool once
more and come back to Lawrence. In the mixed light of the
mostly sleeping neighborhood, parts of his features stand out:
the veined angles of his temples, darkly tanned and lined with
wrinkles; his prominent sclera, rimmed as they always have
been with flushed capillaries; his white palms. He stands with
his hands held face up in front of him, as though testing for
rain. I stand next to him.

In my pocket I have a letter he sent me long ago, right after
he had vanished from our lives, and at this moment I consider
asking him about it. I found it this afternoon in my file in the
basement. But as we stand here in the cooling air I realize that
whatever we could say about it now would have only a distant,
altered bearing on the truth; and more than that, I do not want
to give my brother hope. I finger the envelope in the pocket of
my windbreaker, but do not take it out.

Instead, I realize that what I want him to do is ask me a question. Years ago, in another part of the country, in a place where

there was summer and winter and fall, where there was a humid green spring and families we all knew, he would have taken this moment to teach me something about the world. He would have asked me about the planets, or about electric current, or about the climatic forces that have produced the cottony cirrus clouds now moving above us, bright with suburban light. I look up at them. He was always my teacher in the world, if nothing more, and I was — and still am, in truth — his student.

But he doesn't ask me anything now. He stands with his hands opened toward the sky, not speaking. It is still warm, sixty degrees, though it is past ten o'clock. In California it is harder to keep track of years. What has happened in those since we have seen each other? Upstairs my son is sleeping, and a few rooms away my wife — my wife! — is readying a few last things for the night. A swimming pool laps at our feet. All around, head-high cypresses hide us.

"Lawrence," I finally say, "what is the atomic number of chlorine?"

"What?"

"The atomic number of chlorine?"

"Of chlorine," he says. He studies his palms. I think of him, standing in a gray uniform at the exit door of a casino, shiny black stripe down his pants leg, jingle of keys on a chain at his belt, scanning the tables, lights flashing all around him — Bingo! Play! Slots! — his billed cap slanted back and one hand in his pocket. He looks up. "Seventeen," he says.

"Right," I say. "Bingo."

He turns away from me. "Can I go in the water?"

"Go ahead."

He steps quickly out of my shoes, pulls off my shirt and pants, folds them, more carefully than I thought he would have, and sets them on the deck. In my white underwear he steps forward to the side of the pool. He is thin and without clothes looks taller: the interior structures of his body — the winglike ilia, the long femurs — are even more evident in the shadowy light. He bends and dives.

I remember that he never learned to swim well, never was an athlete, and now in the pool he splashes, sinking and rising, gulping harshly. He moves in uncoordinated strides from wall to wall, his huge mass of hair plastered back and shiny, like an animal's. He drops his head below the surface. When it comes up he spits a stream of water, inhales heavily, and drops it under once more. Then he swims again, wall to wall to wall, kicking off the tile rim at one end and reaching for it with his good hand at the other. He always had an inhuman energy, and now I stand at the pool's edge and count twenty-seven laps before he rises up in the shallow end, climbs out, and squats on the cement. I go to the pool house, where I keep a change of clothing, and bring him underwear and a towel.

He dries off. Carefully he replaces his clothes, handing me his heavy, soaked underwear before he puts on the set I have handed him. The way he dons the shirt, patting each button after fastening it, running his fingers around the collar crease, fills me with regret. He yanks sharply on the tails before pulling the pants up around them, slides the fly up to the last zipper notch, tightens the belt, and adjusts the big brass buckle so that it sits on center. He double-knots the shoes.

"Can I stay for a few days?" he asks.

I look at him. I scratch my palm. In the house the light has come on in our bedroom. "No," I say. "You can't."

He pats the wet net of his beard. "I thought you might say that." He glances away. "Your wife said it was fine with her."

"I'm sorry."

"Are you?"

"Yes."

I look down. I wonder what his place in Reno is like. Probably no more than a room somewhere, at the top of a residence hall, the ceiling blinking with the neon outside, the window looking over a parking lot and perhaps, in the distance, a small mountain vista. He would have a bed and a bureau, two or three bookshelves stacked with science texts and several years of magazine subscriptions. Down the hall the showgirls would live.

In my wallet are ten twenty-dollar bills from the automatic teller, and I reach back and take them out. They are crisp, and the clothlike stiffness of the paper makes it seem as though I am giving my brother something of value. "There's a bus at midnight," I say. "I'll take you there."

He looks at the money. "Hey," he says, "not bad."

"Do you need more?"

"Do I need more? Everybody always needs more."

"I'll drive you to the bus."

It is close to eleven by now. Around the neighborhood, lights have gone out. Lawrence folds the bills one at a time, creasing them neatly, and slides them into his breast pocket. With his fingers he combs back his wet hair and, leaning forward, squeezes a small stream of water from his beard. We go inside, where he repacks his small duffel, and then I put Abraham on his leash and we get into the car. The dog, his shiny pelt quivering, bounds and paces in the back seat, sniffing the late night air, while Lawrence sets his bag on the carpet next to the gearshift and pats it down. I start the car and we slide out of the driveway onto the hilly streets that lead into town.

This time I don't bother taking a different route. We drive straight through our neighborhood, the Land Cruiser's yellow headlights picking up the shining crescents of stucco porticos like white half moons amid the black iron of the gates. Flood lamps light Moorish balconies draped with bougainvillea. We move steadily downhill along the curving, palm-hung streets until the road begins to flatten, then becomes straight, the trees less densely planted now and the houses squatter, exposed across their small square yards and sitting close up to the street. He looks out the window.

The bus station is five miles away, a one-story building outfitted with travel posters above the counter, a wall-length window, and blue plastic chairs that face the lot. It occurs to me only at this moment that Lawrence has left without saying goodbye to Elizabeth or Jonathan, has simply set his clothes into his neat duffel and come with me now, dressed in my own, no more resistant than a child. Next to me he bobs his head slightly.

"Lawrence," I say, "what made you decide to come visit?"

"What made me decide? I don't know. I figured now was a good time," he says. "Time comes around." He smoothes his jeans with his palms. "I'm in a little bit of trouble."

"What kind of trouble?"

"Just a little bit, nothing big. A little bit of trouble."

"So you decided to visit?"

He nods. "I figured we'd both forgotten everything."

I open my window. "What was it that *you* were supposed to forget?"

I look at him; he is adjusting the buttons on his cuff. He could answer me, I realize, but his skin has the sallow paleness of a man older than his years, and I know he will be silent. He closes his eyes, keeps them closed a moment, then opens them. "It's funny," he says, "that you're taking me to the bus again." He smiles slightly.

"This is the station," I say. "I'll wait with you."

We get out of the car. The smells here on the lot, of diesel exhaust and the antiseptic floor cleanser and, next to me, the mix of chlorine and clothes soap that comes from my brother, make me think of all these near attempts: of Lawrence; of the fat Indian woman behind the ticket counter, trying to make the bus station as clean and optimistic as an airport; of the buses themselves, tint-windowed and aerodynamic, but still buses. They roll up onto the blacktop. There they wait, parked beneath flipping signs, their engines rumbling. The doors hiss, shake, slide open. The Reno bus pulls in.

I leave Lawrence outside and go in to buy a ticket. "Have a pleasant trip," the cashier says. She smiles. "And good luck."

He is sitting on the curb when I come out. When he sees me, he stands and brushes the back of his pants as if to apologize for dirtying them. I stand next to him.

"That's your bus," I say.

"I guess it is."

We stand there without talking. In the bus's curved brown window, I watch the two of us. We are wearing the same thing, more or less, blue jeans and a button shirt. But what is it about him — the boniness of his build? the harsh, excited features? — that makes him look this ragged. He climbs onto the first step of the coach before he turns around to face me, and when we embrace he is leaning over so that only our shoulders and cheeks touch, his beard softer than I imagined it, as it had been that morning.

"Goodbye, Lawrence," I say.

"Edward," he answers.

"Good luck."

The door closes, bouncing on its pneumatic hinges, and I walk back to the Land Cruiser. Abraham is in the front seat. I watch my brother through the bus windows, his head ducked, moving down the aisle, stopping here and there at seats as though he can't decide on one. Finally, near the back, he chooses, and then turns his bearded face toward me. We look across the lot at each other, his neck bent toward me, my own head leaning back against the leather rest. Abraham sits forward on his haunches.

When the bus pulls out of the lot I wait a moment, then start the engine. I open the passenger window an inch. Abraham puts his snout into the wind, and together, staying back a block, hiding behind other cars, we follow. The bus drives out along the narrow streets of this unfamiliar neighborhood, its black exhaust fuming at each start and stop. When we reach the freeway I don't turn toward home; I stay behind the bus, keeping its lights in view.

The night air is clear. We are heading toward Nevada. The freeway, smooth and new and surrounded by shallow, green hills, rises and dips. There are few cars out at this hour. On the hills, small, suburban houses are lit up, rising in uneven packs toward the low summit. The bus, I know, stops again in twenty miles. I think of Elizabeth and Jonathan. My son is asleep now, dreaming a five-year-old's dreams. He likes Lawrence, likes his misbehavior and — perhaps, I think, moving a hundred yards behind the dim taillights — perhaps he likes the human miscalculations that have emerged now, years later, as Lawrence's small grotesqueries. I am glad of this. There are children who ridicule what is different: I am glad Jonathan is not one of them. Ahead of me the taillights blink and brighten as the driver changes gears. I think of Lawrence, of his bearded, bobbing head against the blue leather seat. Where was I to be loyal? To the fact that we lived together in the same house for fifteen years? That we share blood? Or to Elizabeth and Jonathan, the life we have made ourselves? Behind me, at the end of this road, sleeps my son in cotton pajamas with drawstrings. His house, his parents, his few friends — what he knows about the world is no larger than the oblong funnel of his sight. Ahead of me, his shirt-sleeves too short for the curveless arms they cover, rides my brother. He has come to me now for help and I have denied him, turned him back into a world that has never embraced him. He rides alone. Abraham, next to me, lies down and settles his moist nostrils on the seat.

When the bus reaches its exit we follow. Ahead of us, down the ramp, its lights dim and brighten, exhaust spewing, the driver downshifting toward the stop. The terminal is a one-room concrete building a few blocks off the freeway. When the bus pulls in there I park down the street and turn off my lights, sit with the motor running, the windows down, and Abraham pacing behind me now in the back seat, sit there watching the tall, double-hinged doors of the bus to make sure my brother does not step out of them.

II

WISCONSIN

FOR FOUR YEARS OF OUR LIVES, for the four years in which I truly came to know you, Lawrence, you were a thief and a parking lot hoodlum and a boy our mother talked about while looking into her tea. That was what I knew of you when you were in high school. You didn't steal every day but I know you stole for a long time — for all those years, I believe. De-Niord's Men's Store was your favorite target, the shop on East Hoover Street whose window platforms held mannequins in Windsor-knotted ties and vested suits pinned open at the lapel so that their sewn brand names showed against the silk inlays of the pockets. Eugene deNiord, who owned the store, lived in one of the riverboat houses on the northern edge of Blue River and had been a friend of our father's in the days when our father was still around: Did this have anything to do with it, Lawrence? More than once you came home — whistling and snapping your fingers, grinning just slightly — in a different suit of clothes from the one you had worn to work. This was obvious to me, but our mother never seemed to notice. I sat on the bed in our shared room when you came in from the afterschool shift at deNiord's and took off a new pair of corduroy trousers, belled at the ends, shimmering dully where the nap changed direction. I leaned against the wall as you set them on the bed and pulled out the new belt, holding it by the buckle and guiding it like a snake from the loops. You snapped the pants smartly, folded them over, and hung them from a hardwood trousers hanger that gripped the cuffs and held the pants upside down. The hanger must have been stolen from deNiord's as well. I tell you this now because I want you to know that I was impressed with the things you did: perhaps you were not a hero to me, Lawrence, but in my life I did see you as a guide. My own pants were blue jeans and a pair of corduroy straightlegs rubbed down to the undercloth, and all four pairs lay rolled up in the bottom drawer of my dresser. I owned one shirt with buttons and hadn't yet imagined the day when my own clothing would hang upside down.

You took off your shirt next. You unfastened the buttons with your right hand, snapping your fingers over them in a one-handed maneuver that had some of the deceptive, open-palmed flourish of a magic trick. Your bad hand stayed behind you and your gaze remained placidly in the middle distance. The shirt fell open across your chest. You removed it, folded it back while holding the shoulders, hung it in the closet, and rebuttoned it there. The row of hangers shuffled and clicked. I'm not sure how I knew that many of your clothes were stolen — I don't believe you ever told me. It was a small point of respect between us and a lesson about unsaid things. I nodded at you when you undressed, smiled at the particularly nice pieces you brought home. We kept the closet door closed. You stole hats, mittens, and socks; you stole sweaters and umbrellas; you stole an alligator belt and a fur-lined leather jacket with epaulets. I watched you, Lawrence. The closet filled up, and now and then when it became too full a whole section vanished. I don't know what you did with those things. On the hanger bar an empty space appeared, which you filled again over a few months before those clothes too, like so many other parts of your life, simply disappeared.

You dressed well, and in Blue River not many other boys did. A town on the high cliffs of the Mississippi River did not require ties or suit jackets. After high school, most of the men ended up at the United Tool plant, where they filled day and night shifts in the huge brown building two miles from our house. The long loading yard was lit up inside the fences at night like a diamond mine. The smokestacks stank of sulfur, and coated the dungarees and flannel shirts of Blue River with a slick yellow dust that made our clothing feel damp. At night, from the small outcroppings above the river, we would look north to where the factory glowed like an eternal fire just beyond our view, the smokestacks throwing luminous white clouds into the air. From that vantage point we could look up or down the curving bend of dark water that moved below us, loaded with the silt of Minnesota and northern Wisconsin, and then disappeared south into Iowa and Illinois. From there, beyond our view, the brown water slid the rest of the way downhill, unimaginable tons of it, all the way off the continent into the Gulf of Mexico.

During the years you were in high school — fighting, stealing, soaking the bloodied knuckles of your right hand in bowls of hot water and garlic — during those years you dressed like the mayor of the town, while our mother sat with Mrs. Silver on our porch and prayed for you. Mrs. Silver was her best friend and practically another parent to the three of us; your transgressions seemed to pain her the way they did our mother, like darts. You were running wild then, Lawrence. You wore shirts that nipped at the waist and flared at the shoulders; your eyes stayed half-closed through the day and your breath smelled of smoke. Several times I saw your blood, darker than I thought it would be, mixed — though I didn't realize it then — with the dust on your skin, with the dirt from sandlots where you brawled. You came home with your cheeks swollen and the knuckles of your right hand split, the blood there clotted in uneven clumps around the pale, thick tendon you once showed me sliding underneath. You taught me that day exactly what we were looking at — *extensor digitorum longus*, you said, pulling out your *Gray's Anatomy* and pointing at the page, lifting and clenching your scabbing finger. Your left hand, meanwhile, stayed behind you. You once told me that you never struck with that hand in a fight, although I wonder now what made you so careful with it. What did it mean to you in the end — the shiny thumb more or less normal but the two fat digits as short as pinkies, tapering from the slick-skinned knuckles to the miniature nails. It was a claw. You walked with it in your pocket. It had come from the tranquilizers our mother had taken when she was pregnant with you, although she once told me that it was, in fact, our father's legacy; she said it was how he lived on in our lives. When I asked her what she meant, she said, "Because it is cloven."

The day you showed me the tendon in your hand I remember thinking your blood was dark for other reasons: I thought mine would turn that color too, would lose the rose-petal hue it had then, seeping from my ankles where they brushed along the river brambles. I thought that, like everything else about me — my arms and shoulders, which were starting to reveal an outline, my adam's apple, which had descended and protruded in my throat, my hair, which had lost the embarrassing sheen of a girl's and taken on the coarse quality of your own — I thought that my blood as well would one day be like yours. I thought it changed color with age.

Perhaps I did not know much about you, Lawrence. Perhaps I thought it was normal for a boy with scars on his cheeks and a pair of brass knuckles under his mattress to own a microscope and a textbook of anatomy. It never once seemed odd to me. Perhaps I will never know the extent of your adventures, either — for by the time I truly became interested in your life, you had left us, and I could only look back at a few moments when the fog around what I took to be your glory parted for a moment. Only later did I try to reconstruct your days.

In high school you used to go to parties at which undreamable things happened, a fact I know because, at the age of eleven, I wandered into one. It was at the house of Swede Derman, your linebacker friend whom I had once seen pull a sapling tree out of the ground with his bare hands. When the two of you came to our house together, you drank whole bottles of milk from the refrigerator, and I kept a distance. Swede had crew-cut hair, red skin, and a face as wide as it was high, and part of the reason I kept my distance was that I didn't know whether Swede was his given name or a nickname that only his friends called him. I was very conscious in those days of what I wasn't supposed to do.

I went over to Swede's house because our mother had asked me to fetch you. I don't remember what the problem was — perhaps a pipe was leaking in our basement; perhaps she needed help rearranging the furniture — but for whatever reason, I was full of importance at being sent. I rode my bicycle to the house, which stood at the northern end of town where the street widened at the highway. Rain had fallen that afternoon and my tires hissed. Why did our mother send me on such an errand? Did she know what I would find? Was this supposed to be her warning to me, some kind of lesson that in her misunderstood scheme of things would have turned me against your ways and not, as it actually did, make me a disciple of them? You must have known, Lawrence, that I loved you.

It was ten o'clock on a night full of stars. When I reached Swede's house I set my bicycle across the street and stood for several minutes on the huge lawn that was lit only by the pale flicker of candles in the upstairs windows. I stood with my arms behind me, trying to look relaxed while summoning my courage. Then I ran my hands through my hair the way I had often seen you do, crossed the lawn onto the porch, knocked, waited, brushed back my hair another time, and went in. Until this time, I had never seen you in any social surroundings, in any significant situation in the wide world beyond ours at home, and as I moved up the stairs to the second floor I became acutely afraid of seeing you under circumstances that would change you somehow, that would show you to be not the same as I had thought. Why at that age was I already afraid of that? At the landing I paused, glanced around, took my wallet from my pocket, and set it behind a short wooden bench against the wall — I was wise, in certain ways, beyond my years — then continued up to the top story, where soft, foreign-sounding music came from behind a door. I smelled smoke. Along the baseboards several candles burned in jars, and in their light I could make out the general layout of the hallway. I was still afraid of finding you. It was possible you would be angry. And what if I encountered Swede? I thought of the tree, uprooted and dropping bits of earth.

I peeked in the first doorway and found it empty, which gave me courage to step down the hall toward the second; inside I found a dark room lit only by the faint cast of a candle, and in its flickering shadow I stood trembling. Along the walls I made out two windows, a framed piece of art, and several white shapes, which I assumed were covered chairs, until, squinting in from the door, I realized they were naked girls.

"Who's the kid?" said one of them.

There was a brief commotion and a figure rose from the corner. "Who's the duckling?" came a boy's voice.

"I'm Lawrence's brother."

"Well, take off your clothes."

"I have a message for him."

Another figure rose. What had I seen of the world at that point? I had never fought another boy, never kissed a girl, had not yet tired of stoop baseball and summer fishing for bass; in your *Gray's Anatomy* I had scrutinized breasts and buttocks and the intricate, sectioned drawings labeled *pudendum* in which a woman's body was cut in half like an ant farm; and now in front of me, close enough to touch me — for I never even thought of touching *her* — stood exactly such a woman, her body shining with reflected light like a moon.

"Take 'em off," came the boy's voice again.

Two boys stood in front of me now, and one of them reached forward, took hold of my shoulder, and pulled me into the room. I assented limply — at that point in my life the grip of his hand was as cruel a blow as I had ever been dealt — letting him draw me forward all the way to the wall. "Take 'em off him."

"Lawrence," I said into the room, "it's me."

"No Lawrence here, duckling."

I stepped toward the door but the hand took hold of my shoulder again. "Lawrence."

"Duckling."

"Strip him."

Hands grasped my shoes and calves. I wish I could say I resisted, as I think most boys would have, or that the prospect of undressing in the company of these girls was what led me to lift first one leg and then the other as the fingers tore at my laces and my socks; but that was not it at all — those naked girls did not entice me but scared me. Only your absolute authority, Lawrence, just the thought of your being somewhere in this house, moved me to let them pull at my belt next, and then my corduroys, pushing them to my ankles so that I had to step out of one leg for balance and then stand there, in nothing but my underwear, my arms hanging at my sides. It was simply that I trusted you.

"Well, isn't he sweet," said a girl.

"I'm looking for Lawrence Sellers."

"I don't know about Lawrence Sellers. How about Jack Daniels?"

"I'm looking for my brother."

They pulled me forward and I found myself on the floor against the wall, five or six of them around me, their faces turned intently — I almost thought kindly — toward me, while one of the girls rummaged behind her and offered me a drink from a bottle. I was still in the fifth grade, and in those times fifth-graders had only early, curious inklings about this kind of party. I crossed my arms over my hips.

"Wait a second," one of the girls said. "I know you; you're Lawrence's little brother."

"I have a message for him."

She smiled at me. If I had been a ship in foggy seas she would have been the lighthouse, the pale, upturned half-circle of her teeth in that dark room an expression of such gentleness that in all my later life such a smile would draw me instantly to a woman. I leaned forward and offered her the bottle.

"I think you made a hit, duckling," someone said.

What would have happened that night if you had not come to

the door then? You stood before us in the threshold, and when you knew that I had seen you, you nodded at me and smiled; I stood, and slipped quickly into my pants and shoes. "Mom wanted me to get you," I whispered.

"I'll be home in a bit."

"It's important."

"I'll be home in a bit."

You smiled again, soft-punched me once between the shoulder blades, and walked away down the hall. I was left at the door; I turned back into the room and waved, as if this kind of party were a normal occurrence in my life and my waving arm an everyday goodbye. And though I expected this to be my exit, I saw that the girl who had given me the bottle was standing. She wrapped herself in a blanket and walked downstairs with me, her bare feet slapping on the stairs on which my sneakers squeaked. She walked out onto the porch, where, angling for a goal I had no inkling of, I held the door for her. I stepped ahead onto the lawn.

"You know how to insult a girl, don't you?"

"I do?"

She came forward to the steps. "You didn't even try to kiss me."

"I didn't?"

"What if I said you can't leave until you kiss me?"

I was below her on the grass, Lawrence, two short wooden steps from where she leaned against the wide white column of Swede's entrance. Did she have any idea how young I was? I put my arm forward and lifted my head almost involuntarily, which put me in a position I recognized from football trophies, and then she was moving down the stairs and her warm hands were suddenly against me and she had found my mouth and I was kissing her — my first real kiss, Lawrence! — shy, nervous, ecstatic, eleven years old and puzzled at the cool slide of her tongue inside my mouth. It was a kiss, I now believe, that

you had asked her to give me. The next day you came home
with my wallet.

Meanwhile, with her older son running wild and the teenagers
she counseled at St. Vitus High School getting dirtier, angrier,
more unkempt and unapologetic every year, our mother had
found the Bible. Suddenly they were everywhere in our
house — soft, leather-backed editions, the bindings some shade
between brown and black, the pages gold-edged and shining
dully. They stood side by side on the wicker bookstand on our
screened porch; they rested next to the blue glass ashtrays in
our living room, backs bent, marked with the narrow red ribbons that hung from a rubbery glue inside the spines. Importance emanated from within them: from the text, which was
columnar and separated down the middle by the ghost of a red
line; from the gray Roman numerals, set in the left margin
against the verses; from the translucent white paper that
seemed to release from the right and spring to the left magneti-
cally or electrically as the pages were turned. "Do not think
that I have come to bring peace on earth," I repeated to myself,
trapping a praying mantis against the rotted pine siding beneath the hose bib outside; "I have come not to bring peace but
a sword."

Our mother sat with Mrs. Silver on the porch, identical editions of the Bible open on their skirts, iced tea and, later, the
rose-colored vodka cranberries on the table next to them.
Sometimes Darienne joined them; she felt a faith that you and
I would never know, and that year she had begun her own Bible
study. Everything you ignored in the world, in fact, Darienne
was just beginning to embrace. She had taken up the oboe and
now the Bible, and she was already a painter; upstairs in her

room, she had a music stand, a plate of votive candles, and stacks and stacks of her canvases. Her bed was made with extra blankets so that she could keep all her windows open; next door to her, where you and I slept, the turpentined air that had blown outside from her room blew back into ours.

In those days when I came inside from the yard, I could tell when Darienne and our mother and Mrs. Silver were together on the porch, because the air in the house would be heavy with the smell and feel of women. From the kitchen I could hear the whisper of the Bible pages. Mrs. Silver always looked inside and asked me to sit with them, but I never would: you, I knew, would have felt betrayed. Instead, I went upstairs and opened all the windows until the Mississippi breeze cleaned out our room.

Every now and then, Henry Howland, the principal of St. Vitus High School and a suitor of our mother's, would join them on the porch, and on these days Mrs. Silver would ask anew if I would care to sit with them. I sometimes acquiesced. The porch smelled of his hat and his cigars then, although of course he did not smoke them in our house. He asked me questions about my life, and as I answered they all drank from the tall tumblers that our mother stored in the freezer for occasions. The ice clinked and floated and made fog on the glass. They sipped from straws. After a few minutes of my stories, they nodded, then pulled back the red ribbons and read aloud, their voices flat and incantatory, while the trapped wasps buzzed like alarm clocks against the screens.

But I wanted nothing of religion. I wanted what you came home with, Lawrence: I wanted the smell of smoke and liquor and cologne, and of a certain acrid sweat, like sweetgrass, that meant you'd been in battle. Mrs. Silver, more than anyone, tried to bring me to the church, but I would not come. Instead, I waited for you upstairs, while on the porch they prayed for you to change your ways. Their voices dropped in earnestness.

If you'd been in a scrape, they prayed harder, and on those after-noons I would hear your name, their quiet verses, then your name again, and a flush would rise in me.

Only once had I actually seen you fight. It happened, I re-member, around the time our mother had taken up the Bible, that spring when the air had warmed so quickly it seemed the winter had been ignited and burned away. I was walking home along the palisade. In the parking lot of the old drive-in theater, now dotted with bent and broken transmitter poles, I came across a group of older kids: you were among them. It was dusk. To my left along the river a container ship moved into view. Against the mast lights, which glowed hazily in the mist like torches, the river trailed off, already black, the first part of the landscape to pick up the color of the night. The stars were not yet out. Off to my right stood the teenagers, two groups of them. They faced each other across the lot, walking one step, pausing, then walking another, until amid the cockeyed poles they stopped a few yards apart and exchanged words I couldn't hear. I saw you easily, Lawrence: you were in the gang coming toward me.

The pavement was pocked from years of winter, and in the warm night smelled of urine and new grass, its snow gullies shining in the last glow of the horizon. Across the blacktop you and your friends moved again, long shadows hanging in some hands like snakes. I squatted with my back to the cliff and river, no route there if they saw me, hiding behind a damp clump of grass as my heart moved up into my throat. I knew what you were going to do even before you met in front of me, you and your enemies, not like armies but like dancers. To the left, two of you turned slowly around each other; then another pair, on the other side. You touched first at arm's length, tap-ping your half-clenched hands against each other at the finger-tips only, those fingertips crossing the space between pairs of you with the glancing, downward flight and snapped return of birds' beaks, movements that seemed delicate until those same hands, the dozen sets I watched in the low light, clenched in a single instant, some curious moment of explosion, as though a fuse burning to all of you had touched the gunpowder and a flash ignited everything. You stepped forward and punched and gripped and kicked each other. Blows rang. A boy fell and another was kicking him in the belly and chest, driving him in a circle on the pavement like a can or a rag; another boy crouched nearby, and there in his hand I saw the flash of a blade: the figure facing him turned and sprinted away across the lot. I heard a wail, a scream; the boy across from you had picked up a piece of wood and was slashing it in the air while you backed up, parried, moved sideways on the balls of your feet, your right hand feinting, darting back, the fingers there still open as the wood sliced the air before you; and I thought I saw in your left hand, held behind you and out from your body, a turning, dark shadow, so difficult to see that at first I was not sure of it; and I ran, first the slipping, sandy path under my feet, sinking with each step, then the uneven cut of the lot turning my ankles — I ran toward you until I stood twenty feet onto the asphalt, where in front of me a boy fell and another stood over him, kicking, and suddenly you saw me — I knew you saw me, Lawrence — and at that moment you reached up as the boy in front of you faltered and, shown against cloudlight, you stepped forward and brought down your cocked arm, the chain invisible in flight, nothing more than a weighted hitch in the arc of your hand and shoulder, a motion I would see in dreams and tossed stones the rest of my life.

Indeed that night I did see it in a dream — the quick slice of your arm through the air, not a throw or a swimmer's stroke but the precise, down and forward lunge of a jockey's whip; and that was what you were doing: you were on a horse, your arm lashing again and again against the galloping neck. I woke and calmed myself and breathed deeply several times in the room where you too, six feet from me, were breathing with a chesty calm. I knew that if I came fully awake the dream would not return, and what I thought about in those few minutes as I fought off sleep was the instant when your fury had switched suddenly to violence, how irretrievable that moment was.

The next day Mr. Howland called our mother to say that the school had heard about a troubling incident, and that evening after dinner I heard her talking to you in the kitchen. "Who was with you in that horrible scene?" she said. "Who, Lawrence?"

I was listening from the top of the stairs. I heard Kleenex pulled from the box. "Who?" she said again.

"I have no memory of it," you answered.

There was no blue anywhere in our bend of the river. The Mississippi that flowed by our town was pale brown, and beautiful only on clear nights when the stars shone in its wide, dark stripe between the bluffs. By day, the water was slow-moving and immense and the color of unplanted fields; it traveled, as we were taught, the whole breadth of the country, and in school we saw photographs of its muddy tendrils reaching at last across the Louisiana delta, into the unearthly, tropical blaze of the Gulf of Mexico.

Edge Road, where our house stood, ran west from the center of Blue River until it neared the river cliffs and then twisted south away from town as the houses thinned out. The blacktop on our stretch of road was unstably supported by the sandy cliffs; in places it had given way so that car wheels ran in unpaved grooves. The road arced out toward the river every hundred feet or so, then dipped back landward, where, at the apex of each curve, a house was set. On the river side, most of them were two stories and wooden, with window balconies that looked west over the water and gave them the appearance of riverboats come up onto the land. The ones closer to town had columns on the front porches and intricate wood scrolling on the trim that again made them seem like vessels built for the water and not for the reddish-brown farmer's earth on which they stood.

That earth, nearer toward where we lived, became sandier and grayer, the color of tree bark, and was prone to erosion at the bluffs. The houses around us were half the size and newer, with metal siding treated to resemble wood, iron poles in the yards holding clotheslines, and aluminum roofs so bright that in the summer you could not look at them. We lived almost at the very end of Edge Road, one house from the last and a hundred yards north of where the asphalt ended at the cliff: years ago an engineer had laid a curve too close to the edge, and a slide had taken it. The blacktop had fallen into the Mississippi, and along with a back yard of stringy grass, had begun the slow float to the Gulf of Mexico. Now the road ended right there, its faded center line heading straight out into the air above the river, the asphalt still hanging by its own strength two or three inches past the edge, dropping off in the winter when the snow weighted it and growing again in the summer when the dry earth below it crumbled. Until the Community Club built a fence of concrete and logs there, it was possible to drive a car right off the end of the road into the air.

Our mother had bought the house the year our father left her. The yard was large, but she had got the place cheap because of erosion there. It was a small problem to fix — we just needed to plant deep-rooted grasses and a couple of trees at the advancing edge of the cliff — but that was something we never did. Each year our land was an inch or two shorter, and the Mississippi, which churned quietly at the shore a hundred feet below us, was that much wider.

Our mother had started working after our father left. Mrs. Silver baby-sat for Darienne and me; Lawrence was in the first grade. By the time I started kindergarten, our mother had become the guidance counselor at St. Vitus High School. She wore mid-length flowered dresses and either a bracelet or a necklace but not both, and sat in a car-sized, one-window room where she talked to teenagers in torn white shirts about why they fought. She talked to them about why they robbed, why they flunked, about why they had babies, about what they meant by their angry words, painted at midnight across the red-brown fronts of the buildings. She sent them out carrying buckets and wire brushes to wipe away what they'd written — *I love, I hate, Screw* — and paint what remained with an imitation of brick that was opaque enough to blur their words but not to conceal them. For one or two weeks a year, she substituted for the English teacher, and on a shelf in our living room stood the four books she taught from — *Death of a Salesman, Oliver Twist, Tortilla Flat,* and *Our Town* — next to three leatherbound Bibles and an oil portrait, painted by Darienne, of you and me.

In the summers our mother spent her days with Mrs. Silver, drinking iced tea or vodka cranberries on the back porch, looking over our small vista of river, and thumbing through a church magazine called *The Light*. From *The Light* and her Bible and the newsletters that arrived by mail from other parishes, she amassed the body of knowledge she used to raise us. This knowledge included a good bit of worldly information too, although her wisdom was never hard-kept like yours. I'm sure you remember her little rules as well as I do: the chocolate in chocolate milk undoes the benefits of the milk; water is the best and in fact the only thirst quencher; the fastest way to cool off is to take a hot shower. She made her points whenever she could, but as part of her general devotion would yield on any of them.

You, on the other hand, would yield on nothing. I can to this day recall lists and lists of facts, because my childhood was filled with them — hers and yours, your different bits of information sprinkled over my life like seeds. You used the things you knew to attack the world, to make it give ground, like a boulder yielding to a lever. You knew the mechanics of engines and the forces of weather; you knew that a frozen lake held a pocket of air beneath the ice; that doorframes survived earthquakes; that in an avalanche one should make a swimming motion and ride the tumbling snow like a wave. These facts were your realm and your blessing, the facts of gears and waves and weights of rock.

What was not your realm, however, what was the curse of your character and the seed of your downfall, I now think, was your inability to forget the insults and petty defeats of your life. Grudges grew in you. I forgot my life an hour after it had passed before me, but you kept lists of older boys who had humiliated you, of girls who years ago had shunned you, of drivers who had honked at you unjustly in traffic. Now when I consider your life I see that much of what happened to you arose from this single inability. Of course you cannot have forgotten the time when you were twelve or thirteen and Keris Salmon lured you into skinny dipping along the wooded southern bank of the river, then stole away with your clothing. He took everything but your hat, so that you had to hide in the river till dusk before walking home. This was in the days when you were still a shy boy. Our mother was at the point of panic when you arrived that evening just after dark, naked, trying to walk slowly, shivering, biting your lip, your hat set low to hide your eyes. The mark of your pride, our mother said, was that you walked home slowly. Never mind that you waited until dark: that was prudence. You wrapped yourself in a towel without saying anything and went upstairs to change. For years this was the story we told when you were not present, the story that explained you — my cold, proud, naked brother walking home in the dark.

Perhaps you shared this characteristic with our mother; perhaps the inability to let go of her grudges was what led her to religion. It was faith, after all, that at last allowed her to forget the one great injustice of her own life — our father was somewhere in New Mexico or Texas — as well as the small tribulations that in our childhood had loomed in our house like clouds. Once when she had been sold an inferior roast she brooded for two days, then the next night brought it back and left it, raw but already spiced and poked with a fork for tenderness, on the hood of the butcher's car. Another time, when she had bought an underfrosted cake from the Cavanaugh Baking Company, she parked her car on the sidewalk in front of the plant door until Anne Cavanaugh herself came outside with a set of frosting bellows. Our mother did things like that; then, when she found the Bible, she stopped. Religion at last allowed her to see her life as I think I have always seen mine — as taking place from that day forward and not that day back — although it was also, I believe, her place of retreat from us. From *you*, I should say. Maybe this was why she tried to convert you but never me. This was an odd fact of our household. Only Mrs. Silver seemed to take an interest in giving me religion, and I think she did this more from fairness than from desire. Our mother, on the other hand, talked to you in a low voice about God whenever she could — cutting squash at the sink while you sat staring out the kitchen window into the yard, filling a lime pie on the counter while you ate your lunch from the open refrigerator. You would listen to her for as long as you could take it, and then you would walk away.

Sometimes, especially when she had cooked something you didn't like, you would start an argument about it. I now think that you did maintain a certain kind of faith — there was a surety to your thought that could not have arisen without it — but in those days you gloated with your utter godlessness.

"All right," I remember you saying to all of us one night while we ate macaroni with bread crumbs, "give me one example of a miracle."

Our mother took a bite of the macaroni, which crackled. Mrs. Silver poured iced tea into her glass.

"Oh, Lawrence," said our mother, "you cause us such sadness."

"Us? Who's us?"

"Your family and me."

"That's right," said Darienne. That afternoon she had gone to Bible study. "All of us."

"He's not causing me sadness," I said.

"Shut up, Edward."

I opened my palms to her. "Is that what they teach you in Bible study, Dary?"

"Lawrence is causing all of us sadness," she answered. "And you are too, Edward." She nodded at me. "And God is sad too."

"Wait a second," you said. "I'm causing *God* sadness?" You poked your finger at your own chest. "God is sad about Lawrence Sellers asking for some proof? What's the theological basis for that one?"

"Don't exaggerate, Lawrence." Darienne looked at our mother. Nobody liked to argue with you, especially about logic.

"Perhaps you *are* causing Him sadness," our mother said, "in a general way. We're all part of His flock."

"Okay, let me get this straight," you said. "Because of me, everybody is sad. God is sad. The Egyptians are sad, the Ethiopians are sad."

"Don't exaggerate, Lawrence."

You looked around the table. "Okay, don't be sad; just give me one example of a miracle."

"If you need an example, then I'm afraid you will always miss the bliss of faith," said our mother.

"That's right," said Mrs. Silver. "God is the point where logic fails us." She smiled benignly. "He is the point beyond the far edge of the universe, at the moment before time begins."

"And He's supposed to appear in blinding light. Am I correct?" you said.

"Sometimes He does," said our mother. "Not always."

"Come on," I said. "How about a small miracle, just so we can talk about it?"

"There is no miracle too small to satisfy the faithful," said our mother, "and none great enough to convince the skeptics."

"Well put," said Mrs. Silver.

"The Shroud of Turin," said Darienne.

"What?"

"The Shroud of Turin," she said again, looking at our mother.

"Wonderful, honey. That's a wonderful example."

"Pray tell what is," I said.

"It's the shroud they buried Jesus in. When He was resurrected, the light of His soul burned His image into the cloth."

"Hah!" barked Lawrence.

"They have it in a museum in Italy, Lawrence."

"They have lots of things in museums."

"They've done scientific tests that prove it was the flash of His soul leaving His body."

"Hah!"

"They proved it."

"They haven't proved anything."

"Listen, you two," said our mother. "A miracle I can prove is that we are all a family, and we all love each other."

"Amen," said Mrs. Silver.

"Hah!"

You lived so much by your reason, I now understand, that you could never have acknowledged your faith; and I, until much later, until long after you had left us, was the same. Even now I cannot wholly find it — perhaps because, in those days, I always took your side. I know that in return you took it on yourself to teach me about the world, and I am grateful for this, Lawrence. One morning at breakfast with Darienne and me you swallowed a forkful of pancakes, then abruptly gripped your throat with both hands. "I'm choking," you whispered, fumbling with the buttons of your collar and blinking your eyes while Darienne ran to you and shook your shoulder. By then you had begun to slump in your chair. "Do something, Ed," you whispered. I lifted you but you slumped further, and I tried to get my thin arms around your chest to squeeze the way I half-remembered from first aid films. Your eyes closed and you slid sideways to the edge of the chair, then from there onto the floor, where you whispered, "And so I die from a bite of pancake," before you stood suddenly, opened your eyes, and explained to me that anybody who could speak was not truly choking. "If the trachea is blocked," you said, "a person can't make any noise. If someone tells you he's choking, you can relax." The things you taught me were all like that, Lawrence: practical bits about the world that distilled it to its scientific elements. They would give me an advantage, you said, when I needed one.

Mrs. Silver, on the other hand, always taught a different kind of lesson, waiting for those moments when you were not there and then acting, perhaps, in place of our mother. She had taken it on herself to teach me morality. In our back yard, on the porch, on the dew-dampened streets when I walked with her to the store with her two-wheeled grocery cart, she told me stories that were supposed to be funny and moralistic at the same time. She laughed in different ways, depending on the moral. Sometimes it was only a smile and a quick, nearly silent exhalation, her eyes closed halfway; but occasionally she transformed before me, bending forward at the waist, her hand pressed there, fingers spread outward, while all the mysterious years of her life — the stories we knew and her hidden, changeable age — slid off her as though she had stepped from a pool of water. Her breasts, their compact, triangular ridge, bounced. Tears came. This laugh would continue, diminishing, for a whole minute, going and coming as she stepped lightly around me. It was part of what confused me about her, as if in its robust cheer I suddenly glimpsed Mrs. Silver years ago: at twenty-five on a sun-whitened porch, sipping whiskey sours; at seventeen, dancing the conga in black pumps; at fifteen, wearing dandelion bracelets and smoking thin cigarettes.

On summer mornings when I came out to the porch she would put aside the newspaper and walk with me through the screen door out to the yard, where for the first few moments I could smell the sharpness of the vodka, weak but permeating, from her pores. Then the scent disappeared and there was only the hot smell of summer out there, the mix of dust raised by the gentle river wind and a heat that seemed to come not from the sun but from the brown-edged leaves of the ground weeds themselves. She was short, with small, wet eyes, friendly features, and pale, nearly white skin. We walked in the yards along the river bluff.

"Edward," she said to me one morning during your wild days, "I have a story you need to hear. It's about some men who are under the control of Lucifer." We crossed the narrow strip of bare earth where you had cleared the grass for a drainage gully. I nodded. She picked a dandelion from the hard ground and began pulling the small petals from the head. "There are two groups of starving men — one good and one evil — in his lair, and Lucifer is giving a banquet at which the most delicious soup is served." She paused over the word *Lucifer*. By now, we were walking near the bluff. She stopped and, with her hands in the pockets of her skirt, looked over the divide. She made a habit of hesitating this way, of pausing to let some idea sink in, her small eyes always willing to meet mine, as if somehow I would instinctively know the point of her fable. But I didn't. What were good men doing in Lucifer's den? Below us the water slid toward Louisiana.

"At the banquet," she went on, "the most delicious soup is served. But the Devil has handed out spoons that are longer than the men's arms." She paused again. Into the spiraling wind she dropped a handful of the dandelion petals, which spread skyward in front of us as she waited for me to speak.

"So?"

"So, the men can't eat the soup." She looked at me, her pale cheeks pink with anticipation. "They can't get the ends of the spoons into their mouths." She reached with her arm and pretended to maneuver an overlong spoon toward her lips. "One group of men is shouting; they're tearing out their hair because the Devil's trick has kept them from eating the wonderful soup." She paused. "But the other group — " She smiled, and her voice fell to a whisper. "The *good* men are silent, eating their fill." We walked upriver along the edge of the yard. She smiled again. "How can that be?"

Down from us, shore birds circled over a dark school of bait fish. I looked at her. "They're holding their spoons by the middle of the handle," I said.

"Oh, Edward," she said. "No."

"No, what?"

"That's not the point. They aren't allowed to hold the spoons there. They have to hold them by the ends."

We walked on. "They're not very hungry, then."

"No. They're starving. I already said that."

From inside the house I heard Darienne blow the first notes of her dismal, deliberate scales. I followed Mrs. Silver farther upriver. "Then I give up," I said.

She looked into my eyes. At the apex of each green iris, perfectly symmetric, was a small fleck of black. I glanced away.

"Oh, Edward," she said. "Don't you see?"

"See what?"

She bowed her head toward me. "That the good men are feeding each other," she said.

We walked on. She kept glancing over at me, and finally, when the woods came into view upriver, she stopped. "Do you see the point of my story?" she asked.

"Sure I do."

"What is it?"

I picked up a stone and rocketed it at a bird circling over the river. "It means, be kind to your neighbor."

"Right," she said. "That's most of it." She smoothed her skirt. "But it applies closer to your own life, too, you know."

"I know."

"I'm not sure you do know," she said. She smoothed her skirt again. "The point is that one day you may have to take care of your brother."

While we were growing up, something about our mother doomed her in love. Darienne, whose own amorousness would bloom much later, after you had left us, once told me it was a secret warning signal that she sent out, like sonar. When men ate dinner at our house, she sat forward in her chair so that the back legs lifted off the floor. This overeagerness, Darienne said, was the signal: men fled.

When I consider this, I wonder whether your own conquestial lust was your one-upmanship against her. Of course this is vague speculation, and I do not necessarily believe what you later implied about her, that she had somehow sent you out to avenge our father. I prefer to remember our mother as a placid if somewhat misinformed woman, cheerfully pretty and relentlessly stoic about the wound inflicted by her husband.

The single important man in her life in the years after our father left was Henry Howland, your principal at St. Vitus High School and the breaker, at last, of our mother's will. She saw other men, of course, but after Henry Howland, as you no doubt recall, she more or less let go of her wishes. During your junior year in high school he became a regular presence in our house: he came for dinner a couple of times a week, and at these meals we ate beef stroganoff or chicken cacciatore instead of macaroni or rice casserole. When our mother insisted, Mr. Howland brought over his daughter, Lottie, in her wheelchair. I would not know for many years what meningitis was, and the pity and dread I felt were as much for him as for her: it seemed to indicate something about Mr. Howland himself, that his daughter was partly deaf and her legs paralyzed. She always sat next to me, and at dinner, while our mother made overly cheerful talk about St. Vitus, I watched the small, curled shapes of her thighs beneath the plaid blanket on her wheelchair. After dinner Mr. Howland would open a black attaché case on the tablecloth, and he and our mother would drink tea and talk about school while Darienne and I washed the dishes and Lottie watched TV in the living room with her mouth open. You were always absent: you ate before Mr. Howland came over and stayed out of the kitchen while he was there.

Before Henry Howland there had been a small number of other men. Do you recall that, for a few months the year before, she had been seeing Mr. Burrows? He worked at a large desk in the lobby of the First Wisconsin Bank, and from Barbara's Creamery across the square I sometimes sat and watched him through the window. He was heavily built and loose in the flesh around his chin and dark eyes, and he always folded his suit jacket and set it inside-out on the desk to work in his shirt-sleeves. I tried to see him as our father. I imagined him with our mother, driving to La Crosse for dinner by candlelight, or standing along the aluminum rail of a mock paddlewheeler from the River Dream Fleet. I imagined him kissing her. At our house he breathed hoarsely and ate heavily, although I liked him because the first time he came he brought a baseball glove, and after dinner went outside with me to play catch in the yard. But Mr. Burrows vanished the way all the other men in our mother's life had, with a flourish. On their last date, you may remember, he'd taken all of us to La Belle Fleur, the only expensive restaurant within fifty miles of Blue River. After that night he stopped coming by our house and I began to feel ashamed every time I saw him in the window of the bank, ashamed that I'd ever imagined him as anything more than a heavyset, hard-breathing man with a brass-and-marble nameplate on his desk.

For a while, our mother had also seen Mr. deNiord, the man who had given you the job at his clothing store. He brought her a blouse or a scarf each time he visited, and one day after they'd been out a few times together he arrived at our house with earrings for Darienne and corduroy sport coats for both you and me, although of course you already had one in your closet. That flourish was *his* last, and I began crossing the street downtown whenever I passed deNiord's. I didn't mind the men in our house — they smelled of cigarettes and gave our mother a quiet keenness we all could feel. I hoped — I even prayed — that she would find someone.

But after Henry Howland, I no longer believed that she would. It is my guess, Lawrence, that they had an earnest and respectful love affair for more than a year, and I see no reason to believe he was not honorable with her. Of course, our mother and I have never discussed this, but she grew easy during that time in a way she never had before, whistling over the salad bowl while he did paperwork at our kitchen table, or sitting on the sheet-covered couch without her Bible and simply watching him. She became more playful also, which made her seem younger. I remember sitting with her one summer afternoon on the eave of our roof with water balloons in our laps as Mr. Howland turned the corner and came whistling up the street.

But he too, as you know, disappeared as suddenly as the others. The last night of their courtship our mother cooked lamb at our house, a dish that even then I knew we could not afford. It was a Sunday. In the kitchen her tape of Strauss waltzes was playing on the reel-to-reel machine borrowed from the school's audiovisual closet, and in the living room she had pulled the sheets off the furniture. Her hair was pinned in a bun with a turquoise-handled stickpin, and after she served the lamb she took off her apron, left the kitchen, and stayed away a few minutes while I tried to talk with Mr. Howland. Finally, she returned in her blue-flowered dress, and suddenly the air smelled of perfume. I ate the lamb smothered in mint jelly and tried to keep my eyes off her. After dinner, instead of sitting in the kitchen as they usually did, they left to go somewhere. Where do you think they went, Lawrence? To his house? To a motel? For a walk? It is still difficult to imagine our mother in a love affair. But only a few hours later, she returned, went immediately up to her bedroom, and closed the door, and for the first time in my life I heard her crying.

I got out of bed and went to talk to you in the kitchen. "What's going on?" I said.

"He's dropped her."

"How do you know?"

"It's what men do to her."

"Mom's nice, Lawrence. She's still pretty."

"Doesn't matter."

"Yes, it does."

You reached into the cabinet above the refrigerator and pulled down the bottle of sherry. "Open your eyes, Ed."

"They're wide open, Lawrence." You drank and set the bottle in front of me, where I closed it. "Mold's going to grow in that."

"It won't be around long enough." You drank from it again and set it back above the refrigerator. "Howland's not interested in Mom, Ed. He's interested in cupcake."

"In *what*?"

"Don't be so naïve."

"So why wouldn't he still be seeing her if that's all he wants? He likes Mom. He's just worried about something."

"Open your eyes, man. He's doing it for cupcake, that's one reason." You put your bad hand behind you and faced me. "And he's doing it because he hates *me*."

"What are you talking about?"

"He hates me, Ed, he always has. He's doing it to get back at me."

I opened the refrigerator and looked at the mostly empty shelves. "To get back at *you*?" I said.

"Yes, at me. How much do you want to bet he doesn't see her again after this?"

I took out the bottle of milk and drank from it. "Any amount," I said.

But when our mother stopped crying that night — at one-forty in the morning — I turned off the light next to my bed and finally went to sleep, knowing — for no reason at all except that in every realm I expected you to be right — knowing that she would not see Mr. Howland again. And she didn't. He never again came to our house for dinner; she never again went to his.

Monday morning when I went in to wake her — she had not come out for breakfast — I found her propped in bed, her face so bloodless that at first I thought some physical illness had caused all of this. It was the first time I had ever seen a woman react to news with profound physical change, and certainly it was the first time I had seen our mother truly upset about her own life and not ours. She did not get out of bed that morning, simply stayed there, her head against the wall above her pillow, while I brought her tea and jelly toast. She was sitting in the same position when I stopped in at lunchtime and again after school, the room by then taking on a sharp, unfamiliar smell that made me open the window and wonder again whether her ailment was physical. She would not speak about it. She was flat-voiced in her answers to my questions — more toast? tea? — and it became obvious that it was beyond my character or our relationship for me to ask what had happened. Darienne had to do that, and she did that night after dinner, emerging from the room to tell us upstairs that our mother loathed Henry Howland.

But by the next day, whatever had taken hold of her had disappeared. She woke Tuesday morning, got dressed, and had made our breakfast by the time the three of us came downstairs. She drank her tea and chatted with Darienne about orchestra auditions, which were coming up, and after breakfast set off in her bracing stride toward school. What had happened between her and Mr. Howland? Was it a fight? A failure? Some sad agreement? That evening she told us he was a strong, kind man who had overcome difficult circumstances and deserved our respect and affection from then on. She hoped we would give it to him. Would we? I said yes, as you remember; Darienne said yes. Only you said no.

"The only freedom is in forgiveness," our mother said to you then as you sat across the table from her.

"Well," you said, "in that case I guess I'll never be free." And then, oddly — obediently — you lowered your head.

When I was eleven and you were a junior at St. Vitus, you taught me to classify insects. That spring for a school project I collected hundreds of earwigs and silverfish and slate-gray potato bugs from the moldering pile of grass and leaves in the Bronsons' yard next door. They scrambled in the glovefuls of dirt I sifted over a mayonnaise jar behind the back porch; inside the jar they ran furiously, climbing jerkily up the glass and sliding back into shivering heaps. I collected them mainly so that I would have a reason to borrow your microscope, which sat on your desk in its own locking case and had instructions engraved on its base in German.

I spent hours with that microscope. I loved the sharp yellow background its lamp would suddenly create when the lenses came into alignment, and I loved what you were teaching me; perhaps this was because it separated us from Darienne. The first time I showed her the strange, turned-over sight of the insects' prickly legs and dark underbellies against the glass, she placed her hand on her small breasts and leaned back against the wall of her room. "Edward Sellers," she said softly, fanning her forehead, "you are a cruel tyrant." I laughed. Something about her unusual sympathies always made her seem younger than I was. A fly was buzzing against her wall, and as I stood there she opened all her windows and tried to shoo it out. In one corner of her room stood her easel, propped near the glass so that she could paint the sparrows in our oak, and in another stood her music stand and her black plastic oboe case; I set the jar of insects down on it.

"Pick that up this instant."

I shook it in my hand and the scrambling insects flipped and landed like a pancake. She took hold of the windowsill. "I'll tell you one thing," she whispered; "vermin are not coming into my room."

"They're my project, Dary."

"Well, *my* project is to keep them out of the house."

I clenched my jaw and held the jar up between us, angling its wide bottom so that she could see the hundreds of legs against the glass. I think in some way that you and I were always allied against the women in our family, Lawrence. That evening before dinner when I set down the jar in the pantry, our mother picked it up with a potholder and carried it out through the back door. Darienne sat smiling at me. That night, before going to bed, I went outside with a flashlight. The insects had organized themselves in the jar by species: the fat potato bugs at the bottom; the silverfish in the middle; the earwigs on top. In the flashlight's weak yellow beam, their antennae rose against the glass like wiggling threads.

But the next morning when I came out to the yard, only a few silverfish lay in the bottom of the jar, stiff and barely moving. I leaned down. All the earwigs and potato bugs were gone. The punctured lid lay tightly screwed in place, the cheesecloth top held firmly by its rubber band. This was my first encounter with the mysteries of nature. By then I knew something of the life of insects, that they changed forms in concealed, stupendous ways — caterpillars into butterflies, larvae into wasps — but when I went in to breakfast that morning, I believed I had witnessed a rare demonstration. We ate eggs and rye toast with the crusts cut off, and when I had waited sufficiently long I described what I had seen.

Our mother nodded and smiled, put down her fork as I spoke. "That is a miracle," she said. "A miracle of nature, but a miracle all the same."

Darienne drank a glass of orange juice, set it down, and told me insects could metamorphose through the small holes in cheesecloth or a punctured lid. She took another sip from her glass. "Such was the miraculous tumult of nature," she said. The jar stood outside the screen door to the kitchen, and I watched it while Darienne explained breathtaking escapes in nature: tadpoles in danger turned into frogs and hopped away; flying fish took to the air; imperiled, my insects had returned to their spore stages and evaporated.

You sipped coffee as she spoke. She lifted her hands and flapped them like wings; she returned them to her lap and smiled across the table at me. Then you said, "Bullshit."

I looked at you. At that point I still thought that you and Darienne had been allies for years. "Bullshit," you said again.

"Lawrence," said Darienne.

"My," said our mother.

"My what?" you said. "One of you let those buggers out, and Ed knows it." Then you were quiet. For at least a minute nobody spoke. I looked out the door at the bottle; two silverfish that had appeared dead now hobbled along the perimeter, their hind segments angled away like scorpions'. You stood and left the kitchen.

"Thou shall not take the Lord's name in vain," said our mother.

I looked at her and Darienne, who both had their hands folded on the tablecloth. "I didn't hear God's name in there," I said. I let out my breath. "I heard something else, but not His name." Then I looked at my plate while our mother, who was rarely at a loss for words, wound her watch.

"You may be excused," she finally said, softly.

I stood and went out to find you in the yard. I pulled the cheesecloth from the bottle and let the silverfish fall out onto the dirt by your feet, where they lay still for a minute before a few of them crawled away.

You looked at me intensely, as if measuring some hidden capability. "Edward," you said, "we're going to make you a real science project."

"I know where I can get a million bugs."

"I know," you said, "but you can do a peckerweight more than just collect the bugs from some old lady's pile of leaves. We'll classify them. That's what we'll do. Classification is the basis of natural science." You raised your eyebrows and I raised mine back. Then you told me that you were going to give me a scientific education.

That fall you did. "Science is predictable," you said to me a few days later. I had come upstairs while Darienne was out and we had wandered into her room together. Her canvases lay stacked against the baseboards. Every painting we could see was a still life involving four oranges: they lay primly on a blue bowl or were scattered on a flowered tablecloth or were balanced on the white wicker arms of our mother's chair out back.

You picked one up and held it to the light. "Science is predictable," you said, "so you can use it to an advantage."

"Be careful of those."

You glanced at me. "This is the start of your scientific education."

"Sorry."

"I mean, look at this." You held the canvas in front of me.

"Oranges." You reached into one of the piles and yanked out another one from the middle, so fast the ones next to it barely shifted. You held it up. "What's this?" you asked.

"Oranges, too."

"What's the difference between them?"

I thought for a moment. "You scratched one," I said. I laughed, and you glanced at me again. I cleared my throat. "There isn't much difference."

"But there *is*," you said. "The light is different, the shape of the oranges is different. In this one they're the same size, but in this one the left one is bigger." You set the two paintings down. "So, what good does that do?"

"I see what you mean."

"That's what your sister calls art," you said. "Drawing oranges in so many ways you can't recognize them anymore. But what good does that do?"

"You're right."

"Art." You chuckled. "Art." You put your left hand behind you. "For Leonardo da Vinci," you said, "art was an important thing, but what Darienne does" — you paused — "what Darienne does is indulgence." You tapped your thigh. "*Self-*indulgence."

"Leonardo da Vinci invented the helicopter."

"Right, Ed. He invented the submarine, too." You looked at me significantly. "And da Vinci wasn't doing art just because he couldn't fit in." Then you put your hand into your pocket and pulled out an aspirin bottle, and when you opened and tilted it, a housefly fell onto your palm. "Now," you said. "What would you call this?"

"A fly."

You reached into your other pocket and emptied another aspirin bottle onto the same palm. Side by side in your misshapen hand were two flies. I peered at them. The second one had a green, iridescent body and legs that were mottled with back-slanting barbs. "Now, what would you call this one?"

"It's a fly too."

"They can't both be flies."

"Why not?"

"Because what does that word mean then, *fly*?"

"But those are both flies, Lawrence."

"Listen," you said, "starting today, you're going to learn to talk about the world accurately. Unlike painting," you said, "this will do you some good."

"One of them's a green fly," I said.

"Order Diptera," you said then. "Division Schizophora."

I looked at your hand. I am now a physician, I believe, because of you.

"Say that," you said. "Say, order Diptera, division Schizophora."

"Order Diptera, division Schizophora."

"Family Muscidae," you said. "Family Calliphoridae."

"Family Muscidae. Family Calliphoridae."

"One of these is a housefly," you said. "The black one. It's called *Musca domestica*." You shook your palm. "The other's a blowfly. *Phaenicia sericata*."

"The green one."

"That's right. They're both in the order Diptera and the division Schizophora, but they're in different families." You opened your palm and we looked into it. The flies were sprinkled with aspirin powder. "We could be in the Sahara desert, Edward," you said, "and you could be in the Ibo tribe, and I could say '*Phaenicia sericata*' and you would picture this little green blowfly, and I could say '*Musca domestica*' and you would picture this black housefly." You smiled at me.

"Wow," I said.

"With art," you said, "there's no way you could do that."

That week, you helped me make a mounted display of the Shield-Backed Beetles. We went out into the leaf pile again, and instead of scooping everything into jars, I searched out just the Shield Backs and lured twelve of them into the small glass chemistry vial in which you had placed a cotton patch soaked in ethyl cyanate. Once the cork lid was tamped down they moved jerkily on the walls, then calmly, then stuporously. When they died we removed them and pinned them onto cork pads according to directions you read aloud to me from a book you had brought home from school, *World of Insects*. I set them in rows of three, arranged by size, and pinned each through the crackly shell and along the last extended segment of the legs. *Order Hemiptera*, I wrote in Magic Marker across a taped index card. *Superfamily Scutelleroidea, Family Scutelleridae*, I went on, though I had no idea of the meanings of these words.

The next day you taught me the scheme of biological classification. "King Philip Come Out For God's Sake," I repeated under my breath: *Kingdom, Phylum, Class, Order, Family, Genus, Species*. "Phylum Arthropoda," I recited to you while you held the book open at your desk, "Class Insecta. Order Protura, Order Thysanura, Order Collembola."

Was this education a kind of commerce to you, Lawrence? Did it seem to you the only respectable part of your life, the only thing you felt you could teach me? I was young and hugely grateful for anything you gave me, and was willing to pay you by whatever means I could. A few nights later our mother called us downstairs to the kitchen, where we found her in her robe at the table, her hair pulled back severely; Darienne sat next to her, staring straight ahead. Next to Darienne on the floor a small stack of paintings lay on some newspapers.

You and I sat down. I watched our sister for at least a minute while nobody said anything. "If you don't blink, Dary," I said finally, "your eyes will dry out."

"Please, Edward," said our mother.

"It's true," I said. "The lids will stick open." I pretended my own eyes were stuck and tried to close them. You laughed, I remember. Darienne didn't, but she blinked twice.

Our mother put both her hands flat on her thighs. "I'm afraid something unpleasant has happened," she said. Darienne looked at her. Our mother cleared her throat. "It's important to remember that we are a family," she continued. "Is there anything more important than that?"

She seemed to be addressing me. I glanced at you. I had the suspicion there *were* things more important than family, and that you expected me to know what they were. While we'd been pinning the Shield Backs we'd talked about how important it was to be rigorously observant, how the scientist's creed was paramount to progress. I looked back at our mother. She was tilting her face forward as though to find a scent in the air. "Well," she said, "is there?"

I turned away and winked at you. "No," I said, shaking my head. "There's nothing more important than family."

"Then I'm going to ask you two what happened to something that's very important to your sister, and I know one of you will come forward." She nodded at Darienne, who reached beside her chair and brought up one of her paintings of the oranges: three broad scratches cut across the canvas. When she lowered it, her eyes were wet. "Ruined," she said.

"Well," said our mother.

"Ruined."

"That's terrible, Dary," I said. I pretended to examine the painting, in which the oranges were shaded and lightened in changing mixes of gold and white and red. "That's a beautiful piece of work, Dary. It really is."

She looked halfway toward me. "Do you think so?" she whispered.

"Yes, definitely. And I don't think it's at all ruined."

She looked away again. "Ruined."

"We'd like to know which of you two is responsible," said our mother. She looked at you, held her gaze a moment, then turned to me. There was a hard cast to her face that I had never seen before. I saw that your jaw was set, and I set mine as well.

"Darienne," I said. "I did it."

Our sister's eyes widened. She got up from her chair, placed the scratched canvas in front of me on the table, and left the room.

"How could you, Edward?" said our mother. She got up too. She walked into the living room, then came back to the doorway. "Well," she said, slipping her reading glasses over her ears, "at least you were honest."

You and I were alone at the table. You tapped your fingers to a tune in your head. We looked into each other's eyes for a while, just the two of us, without blinking, without speaking, as I watched your jaw relax and the corners of your mouth slightly, delicately, turn up.

That summer, the one before your senior year, Lyna Melner came into our life. For the rest of our days together her name would serve as a warning to me, although at the time we met her, as you no doubt remember, she seemed to be the farthest thing from trouble. She was in Darienne's class, three years ahead of me and three behind you, a shy girl who came home now and then to sit in our back yard with our sister and draw. The two of them worked on lap easels behind your tool shanty. What, I wonder now, did you think of her in those days? She was quiet around Darienne and utterly silent around the rest of us. Drinking tea on the living room window seat with our sister or joining us all for dinner, she nodded and blushed at questions but didn't answer them. Our mother, out of kindness, stopped asking. "Be kind to her," our mother once said to all of us; "shyness is a sign of grace."

Over the summer and the beginning of the fall we began to stumble on Lyna by surprise, sitting cross-legged and cross-armed on the grass behind our back porch, waiting for Darienne, her red hair pulled back, or standing sideways behind the elm at the end of our yard so that the trunk hid her slender profile completely. At meals you teased her, and most of the time she ate looking at the table. "You don't say, Lyna," you would beam, reaching for the last blueberries in the bowl after dinner. One afternoon while she was waiting for Darienne in our yard, I watched from the window as you brought out your barbells, set them in front of her, and, while she sat with her arms around her knees and her face turned away, did fifty military presses, sweating and cursing. Did you know I saw you do that?

What happened then did not become clear to me until much later, and I have never told you that I know about it. Lyna disappeared from our lives in October, stayed away for November and December and half of January, her absence barely noticed except for the occasional sight of Darienne drawing by herself on our back porch and our mother saying, one Sunday morning at breakfast, "I miss that Lyna Melner." Then one evening in the middle of the month, Lyna walked into the kitchen while we were eating dinner. Snow had fallen that morning and ice ringed the windows and the roof, but Lyna wore just a light coat over her dress and nothing over her legs, and I saw immediately that she was pregnant. Her face was red and touched with frost. You jumped from the table and came back from the other room with a blanket, which you draped over her while our mother brought her to the stove to stand in the steam rising from the tea kettle.

"I'm going away," she said, practically the first sentence she had ever uttered in front of all of us.

"That might be the best thing," said our mother.

"We're going to Chicago," she whispered. A car honked outside and she stepped across the floor, kissed Darienne, and then went out the back door, her broadened hips beneath the coat the last I would ever see of her. The door closed. We all stood at the table but nobody said anything, until at last you sat again and, as I watched you — as we all watched you — began picking at the tin that held the caramelized crust of our mother's pound cake.

After that, Lyna's name was used as a warning. "*Think* about what you're doing," our mother said to me when I broke through the garage roof chasing a beetle. "You'll end up like Lyna Melner." She said this all the time — when I set a porch plank on fire with a magnifying lens, when I forgot the cookie sheet full of insects I had left to dry in the oven. It was a warning that, despite repetition, made its way to my heart. Now I realize that Lyna's leaving was one of the few moments of consequence I had ever known, perhaps the first time I understood that something irrevocable had happened in the small orbit of my life. She was gone from us now, perhaps forever. What would she do in Chicago? Raise her child? Abortions, I found out, were possible, but as far as I could tell they were far from routine, and dangerous as well.

Of course, it immediately occurred to me that it was you, Lawrence, who had impregnated her. Seducing Lyna seemed within your power; I imagined that it would have been easy for you, and I considered your reaction that evening: you had gone to the other room for a blanket.

I began to watch you closely. I began to pay attention to your gestures and words and demeanor, and to follow you through the small acts of your day. For years girls had been drawn to you; you possessed a power with them that I have almost never again encountered in my life. Troubled girls, girls in rubber thongs and motorcycle jackets, girls with bare shoulders, flocked around you. Their wide, sad eyes studied you. Later, you denied this power, but I am sure you once possessed it. How could you not see it? Your charm had never emanated from where I expected it to, not from the color of your eyes, which were blue — but a pale, weak blue, unlike lapis or the sea — and not from the cast of your chin, which was prominent but too sharp to call truly handsome. It didn't come from the Middle Eastern curve of your nose or, in our father's other incarnation, from the olive tinge of your complexion. I noted your features carefully. You were tall but too thin, and when you walked your limbs struck and wandered, one heel slapping the pavement harder than the other, one elbow cocked. You kept your bad hand in your pocket.

But with women your hand didn't seem to matter. With women it even seemed to help. You lived amid their perfumed embraces: in their curious attentions, in their fat-softened arms, in their wide-hipped, forgiving bodies you buried yourself, over and over again. Still in high school, you slept with waitresses and schoolteachers and any number of girls from the University of Wisconsin. I know this, Lawrence. You slept with barmaids and nurses and secretaries. On our family car trips you lingered inside gas stations, talking through the barred windows to the pairs of local girls who tended the night register. In parks you talked to young mothers. In department stores you sauntered across from the scarf-wearing girls at the perfume counter. You smiled, looked down, nodded.

And they followed. Your pale eyes stirred them, Lawrence, made them gaze sidelong down the lengths of bars at you. You kissed women you had just met, slept with women you barely knew. Once, I saw a girl faint in your arms. Your bony features, later half hidden by your near-black beard, calmed as you listened to them, settled softly into your face so that you were like another person. I watched you carefully. Nodding, you leaned forward; you spoke in a low voice, your right hand out on the table between you. That hand was always face up. The other one rested in the pocket of your pants. The girls talked, their faces lit as if their hearts, their real hearts, knew something extraordinary; and like you, they smiled gently. Then came the moment when you took the left hand from your pocket. On the wooden tabletop, on the park bench, on the Formica counter shiny with wiped grease, you rested it, the waxy, creaseless palm held open. The two fingers, half curled, touched gently at their tips. The thumb reposed. A small falter of recognition blew across the girls' faces; I had learned to expect it. I saw a held smile or a missed blink. Then, mysteriously, their resistance lifted. Now in earnest they leaned forward. You pulled the hand back across the table and replaced it in your pocket. From across the bench, from across the countertop, from across the car seat glazed with summer heat, you slid it into its corduroy hiding place; later, soft-eyed, the girls walked outside with you. Your shoulders touched; they parted, touched again. What could be the power of that malformed hand, I wondered. To me it was hideous, pitiable — I cannot deny this to you — and though I still believe that if I could have anything done over in the world it would be those five fingers, that one small quirk of your gestation, I cannot say, Lawrence, that any love or empathy made it look handsome to me. Yet that is what it was to these girls — alluring, somehow. I can't say why.

At home you brought them down to the basement, where in

those days there was only a lamp, a bench, a laundry sink, and the folding bed our mother stored there. Late at night I sometimes met them. They sat in robes on the bench by the lone window. They lay in the bed, blankets pulled up to their chins. I knew that you liked me to visit. I said hello to them, shook their hands in the forthright way you had taught me, even as they lay there with you. These gestures were disarming, you said. I mixed three cups of coffee in the electric pot and handed them out. Perfume filled the air.

Finally, one night after one of these girls had left, I asked you about Lyna Melner. I took a sip of coffee, pretended to be looking at something out the window, and asked you, without turning. You didn't say anything for a few moments while I peered through the glass, and then I heard you swallow a gulp of coffee and set down your cup. "You're old enough to be honest with now," you said.

What more could I have wanted to hear at that point in my life? You knew this, I believe; in some ways you knew a great deal about people. To be older — to be *thought of* as older — was still as much of a goal as I had ever mustered, and when I turned away from the window that night I felt ready to embrace the truth of whatever you had done. The more dastardly your deeds, the better; if you had impregnated poor Lyna Melner, I would have been proud.

"Were you the one?" I said. "You can tell me."

"I can? Well, that's nice of you. Thank you, Ed."

"I mean, if you want to."

You laughed. You tossed your loafer at me and I caught it, smiling. "I didn't do it, Ed," you said. "I wouldn't get near her; she's just a girl." You sipped the coffee. "But I know who did."

"You do?"

The name you mentioned was that of a boy whose family had

left Blue River a few weeks before Lyna did, a scrawny boy with acne who was a good athlete but not well liked. "You know what I did, though, Ed?"

"What?"

"I took care of him."

I looked at you. I was supposed to know what this meant; it was in your voice that I could not ask for more explanation. What were you saying you had done? At the time I assumed you had beaten this other boy, out of loyalty to Lyna or to our sister, although I also considered that you had simply got money from him for the baby. "There's a kind of person," you said, "who'll do that and not take account for it, Ed. I can't stand that, you know — I really can't stand that." You narrowed your eyes at me. "If you do something, Edward," you said, "stand up to it. Stand up to what you do."

This was the first time I had heard you talk of responsibility, Lawrence, and although I suppose I should have asked how you conformed to that standard yourself, I was six years younger and only shook my head in agreement. Perhaps it was the first sign of the profound change you would later make in your life. Such a change, after all, as sudden as it later appeared to us, must have started much earlier, in a smaller and perhaps illusory form.

Soon Lyna was no longer in my thoughts, but I kept my attentions on you anyway. In an effort to see your life more clearly, I began to read the two magazines to which you subscribed, *Popular Mechanics* and a journal called *The Skeptic*. I now see how the knowledge you gained from these magazines armed you against the rest of us, especially against our mother. At night, in the bright light of your desk lamp, you leaned over the pages, your lips moving slightly with the words. From *Popular Mechanics* you copied plans for things that seemed unbuildable to me, like a glider or a one-man submarine that ran on compressed air. You didn't build them but you redrew the plans in your notebook, your precise pencil marks filling pages and pages of the gridded paper.

The Skeptic always interested me more, however. Wrapped in brown paper, it arrived on a lax schedule, sometimes twice a month, sometimes not for an entire season, and consisted of twenty or twenty-five pages that had been typed, photocopied, and stapled together. I thumbed through the back issues in your desk drawer. Each one dealt with a different occult belief, which the authors attacked: extrasensory perception was shown with movie photography to be sleight of hand; flying saucers were exposed as darkroom tricks; Moses parting the Red Sea was explained with lunar charts to coincide with low water from a minus tide. I looked at that article for a long time, trying to be objective about what was written and what our mother would say in response.

Because of the grainy paper and poor copying, however, photographs that were supposed to reveal hidden wires or thumb-sized mirrors sometimes showed only dark gray backgrounds with black arrows pointing at nothing at all. Nonetheless, the articles bore a weight of harsh authority and discipline. To me the existence of linked nets of men united in their skepticism — as different from our mother as human beings could be — transformed the world into something beckoning and large. The magazine was published in New Jersey.

One day, looking through an issue in the desk, I pulled the drawer out too far and found a back compartment hidden by a strip of plywood. Inside the compartment was a bone. It was a foot long, and the shaft flared out at both ends to the notched ball of the joint, which shined porously, like coral. A medicinal smell cut the air. I closed the drawer. In the science room at school a human skeleton hung on a chain, and as I thought of the bone, I tried to picture it there. I opened the drawer again, reached in, and touched it. How was I supposed to know if it was human? I had seen the skulls and jaws of desert animals on the car trips we took to Colorado and Arizona, but those bones were small, the foreheads papery thin and the teeth set in the protruding, snapping rows of the rat-eating creatures whose deaths caused me no concern. Now in your drawer was something else, perhaps a human bone; maybe an arm or a leg. I lifted it. In my hands it rested with a surprisingly light weight, like balsa wood, and for a moment I thought it was fake; but something about the minute, spongelike holes in the shaft made me certain it was authentic. I set it back in place. I closed the drawer and went into the hall bathroom, where I washed my hands with soap. For a minute or two I stood at the top of the stairs, listening to your voice rise and fall in the kitchen. By now I was certain that the bone was human: Why else would you have hidden it? What did you mean, I wondered, when you said that you had *taken care of him*? I practiced smiling a couple of times before I walked down to breakfast.

In school I sat near the skeleton every Tuesday and Thursday and inspected it, appearing all the time to be gazing out the nearby window. The bones in school, I realized the first day I spent looking at them, had none of the pocked whiteness of the one in your drawer and were probably made of plastic. At home I removed yours from the drawer, traced its shape onto a piece of paper, and brought the paper to school, deducing then that it came from a human leg. From the chart thumbtacked to the wall I saw that it was the tibia.

For the first time, Lawrence, I became afraid of you. I sat in school repeating the word in my head while Miss Hardwick talked to us: *tibia, tibia, tibia.* Sitting at the kitchen table one day, doodling on a napkin, I found that I had written it; you were in the yard, and I tore up the napkin and threw half of it away in the kitchen and half in Darienne's room. When the thought of it entered my mind, I tried to push it out. I did multiplication tables when it appeared to me. I did the thirteens and fourteens. At night I awoke, and in your high-pitched exhale I heard it: *tibia*. Between us, hidden in the desk in our dark room, it rested like a moon-colored snake.

Was it ridiculous to imagine that you had been involved in — I could barely call up the word — a murder? More than likely the bone was merely something you'd found. But I was trying to act older, and since Lyna left I had been concerned with consequential events, making more of everything in an effort to see consequence. One day looking out the window at you swinging the hammer beside your shanty, I decided it was up to me to help you out of this situation. You were half in shade, your legs looked thin, and though you used a hammer well there was something awkward in the wide swing of your arm: you seemed defenseless, Lawrence. For all your strength, for all your frightening deeds, you seemed weak.

I reached into the hidden drawer, removed the bone, and tucked one end into my sock. I pulled my pants leg down over the other end and went to the mirror: the small notch of the joint protruded only slightly from the flat part of my shin. I put on my windbreaker and walked downstairs, out the back door, past you, and to the edge of the land. You didn't even notice me. I headed upriver a few yards to the cover of a dip, where I took out the bone and threw it over the cliff. It tumbled and hit the water with a small white splash that I saw but didn't hear, though I was listening, and then it surfaced for a few moments, angling out into the current, before it sank. I walked back and watched you swing the hammer. Later I would wonder about you as the single great misunderstood part of my life, aware that none of us, not our mother nor Darienne nor I, ever saw you for what you truly were, aware that you yourself didn't

either. You simply invented and reinvented your life, Lawrence — if that can be an explanation for a person — as though
the instincts that negotiated the world for everyone else did not
negotiate it for you. To this day such a thought makes me melancholy. The hammer rose, paused, fell. To no purpose that I
could determine, you were pounding a sheet of metal on your
anvil. In those days, I didn't know enough about you to wonder
what your world was like: you were my brother, that was all,
off in the distance ahead of me, and I had just begun to understand that I had to protect you.

You didn't say anything about the missing bone. I waited a day,
then a week, then two weeks. At dinner and in our room at
night I watched you. Several times in my presence you went to
the desk and opened the front drawer, but not far enough to un-
cover the secret shelf. I waited with my response ready. Then
one night I realized you may have thought that it was our
mother who had found your secret, and I knew that I would
have to say something soon. That is why I told you what I'd
done. We were in our room together, getting ready for bed.

"Lawrence," I said, "I found your tibia."

"What?"

I knew the word would impress you. "I found your tibia."

"What'd you do with it?"

"I threw it in the river."

You stood up. At this point a saying of our mother's came to
me. "I did it for your sake," I said.

You walked from your bed to mine and stepped in front of
me, where, with no change in your expression — I will always
remember this — you drew back your arm and hit me across
the face with your fist. You had never hit me before. You held
your hand up and looked at it. After a moment you said, "Jesus,
Ed. I'm sorry."

"You broke my cheekbone."

"You threw my stuff in the river."

"It's swelling."

You sat on the edge of the bed while I fingered the tender bottom of my eye. The skin was already tight.

"I shouldn't have hit you," you said.

"I'm going to have a black eye."

"No, you're not, but I still shouldn't have hit you." You went to the window. "Damn," you said.

"Ow."

"I'll let you hit me."

"No, you won't."

"Slug me, Ed."

"No, thanks."

"Come on, go ahead." You stepped from the window and got to your knees on the floor in front of me. "Hit me in the face, Ed."

"I don't want to."

"What's the matter with you?"

"I don't want to."

You grabbed my hand and balled it into a fist. "Everybody wants to," you said. "Come on, Ed, punch my lights out."

"Let go of me."

"Knock my brains back, Ed. I'll keep my eyes open."

"I don't want to, Lawrence."

"Plug in my toaster, Ed."

"You're crazy, Lawrence."

"Turn my wig around."

"I don't want to."

"You've never hit anybody in your life."

"I don't want to hit you, Lawrence."

"Hah!"

You stood up and walked to the door. "You want to hit me so

bad you don't even know it," you said, and on the way out you turned to face me. Standing in the doorway, you smacked your head against the wooden jamb, first one side, then the other, before you went into the hall, down the stairs, and out to the yard.

That night, as I lay in bed, you came home. In our room I looked at you silently for several minutes while you took off your clothes, walked out to the bathroom, came back, and thumbed through a *Popular Mechanics*. You got up and came over to me. You put both hands on the top of my head. "Jesus Christ," you whispered, your palms resting there. "I'm sorry I did that."

"It didn't hurt that much."

You looked at my face. You went out and came back with a wet washcloth, which you held to my cheeks. You cleaned them and patted them dry. "Ed," you whispered as I lay there. "Oh, Ed."

There was a sweetness to my wound that made me want to keep it a secret from our mother, but by the next morning when I woke my eye had swollen and turned pink on its lower edge. The first moment I stepped into her sight at breakfast she gasped. "What in good creation happened?"

You were standing at the sink, and you turned to look at me. "I have no memory of it," I said.

Our mother was suddenly very still. "What did you say?"

"I said I have no memory of it."

Her hand went to her lips. "Heaven help us," she whispered.

And that evening, as I'm sure you remember, she made some changes. She was a soft-looking woman, our mother was, with rounded arms and rounded cheeks and a way of leaning back as she spoke so that she seemed to be in agreement with everything, even when she was not; but that night her voice was different. Even those times in the kitchen late at night when she

sat with you after you had been brought back to the house by
Sergeant Apt, when she leaned forward in her chair to speak to
you — even at those times, her voice was empty of the hard-
ness that, when I look back on it, might have changed things
for you. She spoke looking into your face. You tapped your feet,
gazed above her out the dark window, clenched and unclenched
your fists. She enunciated with a crisp diction that she practiced and that made some people think she had an English ac-
cent, though we knew from the few elocution lessons she had
given us that she was merely speaking the words forward in her
mouth, where the instruments of speech were more agile. Even
on those nights, though, her voice sounded the way it always
did — crisply pronounced but soft, a voice we might have heard
on WGNN speaking about the Lord from western Illinois.

But this time the sound of it was different, and that night she
sent you from the house. Lying in my bed, I could hear the
harshness of her words. Had you told her the truth? It was
the kind of thing you might have admitted, your hitting me,
the kind of thing you might have permitted yourself to tell
her. When I came downstairs in my nightclothes, the kitchen
smelled of peppermint and berry and of lime that might have
been cologne except it was on your breath as well, Lawrence,
and I knew from the way you were sitting there that something
had changed. You slumped your chin and stared at the wall. I
stood there for several minutes before you turned and squinted
at me. I touched the tender edge of my cheekbone. Nobody
spoke. Then you got up and went into the bathroom, and we
heard you throwing up.

"We are lost in the black of the woods," our mother said into
the air.

She regarded me. On the table between us sat a pack of Sa-
lems and your slim brass lighter. In the bathroom the toilet
flushed and the faucet went on, and while we listened I saw her

face harden. She sat forward in her chair, and when you came out, wiped your lips on your forearm, and took your place at the table again, she spoke to you in this new voice of hers. "Lawrence Sellers," she said, her face thrust forward and both her hands on the table. "You are not dragging your brother down with you. Do you understand me?" She got up from the table and stepped into the doorway. "Do you?"

You were seventeen years old. "Do I what, Mom?"

"Do you understand what I said?"

You lifted your head to her.

"You are not staying in this house tonight," she said. She walked out to the front hall; I heard the door open and our hanging coats ruffle in the breeze.

"Trouble," you said in the kitchen. You put your head in your hands. "A little bit of trouble."

I stepped closer to you. "I didn't tell her, Lawrence."

"A little tiny bit of trouble."

"I swear to God."

"Yeah," you said as you rose from the chair.

"Where are you going to sleep?"

You looked at me but didn't answer, then got up and left the kitchen. I put your cigarettes and lighter in my pocket, and when I went out into the hall our mother was holding the front door open. The chill spring air swept in around us. She set her jaw. "You are never going to get help from us again," she said.

You nodded.

"Say that," she said. "Say, 'I am not going to get help from my family ever again.'"

You looked at me.

"Say that, Lawrence," our mother said again.

"I'll see you, Ed," you said. You stepped through the doorway onto the porch.

I tried to mouth the words *I'll help you* as you turned around and faced us, but our mother closed the door. She fastened the lock and we stood inside the hall, listening to your boots on the steps. "God save us all," she said, once you were gone.

The next morning, Lawrence, I knew where to find you. Drunk or angry or bleeding from your scrapes with kids from Corinth or Despommes, you always hid in the same spot, a field of head-high grass a mile out of town along the river. Because of all the tunnels trampled through the stalks, we called it Animals' Castle. The tunnels opened onto small rooms lit with dusty, filtered light, rooms that I assumed were made by animals until I was in high school and first made my own. As a child I had often gone there to find you. Injured from a fight, you would hunch your shoulders, pull down your eyelids, saunter like a racehorse down to that yellow-green meadow where the cliff dipped low and became like the land of another part of the country — not the cliffs that we knew but a gentle hill that knelt to the water. Sent to find you, I made my way through the dense grass, pushing apart the fronds while around me hordes of grasshoppers took flight like shot springs into the bright air.

But the morning after our mother sent you from the house, I was walking toward Animals' Castle with my finger on my taut cheek when I realized you wouldn't be there. You were seventeen: you would be with a girl somewhere. My heart soared for you then, Lawrence, for my brother who, forced to leave his own house, could find another by nightfall. You knew dozens of girls — perhaps for this very emergency, I would later think — and you would certainly now be with one of them. How foolish I felt, stumbling through the damp weeds looking for you when you were somewhere amid tossed blankets and morning sun and air that smelled of perfume.

Then I parted a clot of stalks and nearly stepped on you. You lay on your side on the ground, your jacket spread over your head, your legs bent up to your chest. Lawrence, I did not understand, and perhaps still do not understand, why you slept there. Was there something in that cold, hidden ground that you desired? When I leaned down and touched your shoulder, you jolted upright. "Friend," I said, "not foe. It's me — Edward."

The damp air had paled your skin to a shiny stiffness that made you look ill. Why had you come here instead of going home with a girl? Perhaps I should have understood right then that I had miscalculated your life, that you were not who I thought you were; but I didn't. I took your cigarettes from my jacket pocket, lit one, and gave it to you. "You look cold," I said.

"Smart cookie, Ed."

I took a cigarette for myself. You watched me work your lighter, a smile hiding at the corners of your lips, and you watched me try to inhale. I sat on the ground next to you. "You know," I said, "I don't think she means it."

"What are you talking about?"

"I don't think Mom means it, about your not coming back." I let out a cloud of smoke. "I think you'll be able to come back in a few days."

You looked at me.

"You know," I said, "I think Mom's changing." I puffed, held the smoke, and blew it out. "I'm old enough to notice."

"You're not old enough to notice anything."

"But I think she's changing."

"Look, Ed," you said. "Mom changed eleven years ago, that's when she changed."

"Oh," I said.

"And I'm not coming back, Ed. I'm never coming back."

But that evening at dinner you did. You walked in just after we sat down and took the place that our mother had set for you, and that night you slept in our room. Early in the morning, while you were still snoring and the sky was blue-black, I woke and crossed to your bed, where in the palest reflection of the hall lamp I watched the breath in your lean cheeks. That day, I had overheard our mother and Mrs. Silver talking about you on the back porch. "Sometimes I just want to look at him and remember him forever," I heard our mother say, "before it happens."

"He has love in his heart," said Mrs. Silver.

I didn't understand what they were talking about, but standing there above your bed I too wanted somehow to burn your image into my memory. Whatever happened, I wanted to remember you as you were that night — in bed, asleep, and at peace.

After that night, things seemed to change for a while, until one evening in November Sergeant Apt phoned to say you had been caught stealing a leather jacket from deNiord's. A block or two away from the store, you were looking into a shop window, adjusting the fit, when deNiord himself walked up behind you. What were you doing, getting caught like that? By then you'd been a successful thief for years. I went with our mother to the police station to see you.

"It was like seeing your whole life change, right in the mirror," you said to me while we sat alone together in the holding room. In the middle of your story, Sergeant Apt entered and said he was trying to get an order from the judge to take you to court as an adult, since your eighteenth birthday was so close.

You pulled at the hairs on your arms as he spoke. The sergeant looked at the two of us and put his thumbs in his belt loops. "Makes you nervous," he said to you. "Don't it, big man?"

"Save it, Apt," you said.

The sergeant laughed. I was relieved that he did, because your saying that to a police officer threw the world into a sudden new light for me. Sergeant Apt laughed again and walked out of the room.

"Wow," I said.

"Anyway," you went on, "deNiord walks up right behind me and I see him in the glass." You were working your fist in the air above the table, watching it open and close. "His face is happy as a pig's, practically grinning. He stands behind me with his legs together like he's got a potato chip up his ass. He's waiting for me to notice him in the window. Of course I see the bastard — he's standing right behind me — but I figure the best thing to do is go right on adjusting the coat. So I do.

" 'Nice jacket,' he says to me.

" 'Thanks, deNiord,' I say, in a low voice. There's nothing in that voice. I say the name flat because that'll scare him. Also, I'm thinking I might belt him." You closed your fist and looked at it.

"You were going to hit Mr. deNiord?"

"He was about two feet behind me and to the left."

"Mom's been crying all afternoon."

"Shit," you whispered. "Shit, shit, shit."

"What are you going to do?"

"Apt's trying to scare me. He can't do anything, though; deNiord was a friend of Dad's."

I looked around. The room had no windows. The door was closed. I leaned forward. "What about all the stuff in your closet?" I whispered. "What happens if they find *that*?"

You nodded.

"If they find that, you're dead."

You nodded again and gave me a steady look; then the door opened and another patrolman came in with our mother. He told us that your disposition was to be decided in a couple of hours when the night captain came on. You didn't look at him. The officer shook his head a couple of times, and his glance went to our mother, who motioned for me to leave. I was the last out the door, and when I looked back you were sitting with your head down.

We drove home. Our mother couldn't find her house keys and I had to open the door with mine while she stood next to me, shaking her purse. We went inside. It was time for dinner, but she took out a blue notebook I had never seen before and made a phone call instead. I listened, and finally figured out that she was talking to Mr. deNiord. "It was a mistake," I heard her say. "He's not staying in this house anymore. It's not going to happen again. I understand the position you're in." She listened for a few moments. "I know that," she said. "And I'm grateful for it." Then she swallowed. "That would be lovely." She lowered her voice. "You're a great man, Frank," she said and hung up.

Her voice sounded as if the air had gone out of her lungs. I went upstairs to our room, opened your closet door, and gazed at the stolen coats and pants. I gathered them all in a bunch, pulled them from the rack, and climbed out onto the roof. It was dark already. I had doubts about what I was doing, Lawrence, but I ignored them. From the edge of the roof I dropped the bundle onto the lawn, climbed into our oak, and from there to the ground. I picked up the clothes again and walked across the yard to the palisade. I stood at the edge for a few minutes, looking over the dark run of the river. Then, one by one, I threw all of them off the edge. In the moonlight the jackets and pants filled like parachutes, tumbled away, and spread themselves

onto the still surface of the water, the arms out, the legs puffed
with air, and drifted away toward Iowa.

And then, when you turned eighteen, like a boiling pot coming
off the fire, you just stopped. You were graduating from St.
Vitus in two months. The day of your birthday, you came home
late from school, stumbling, working your keys for half a minute before you got the front door open. You walked into the living room, shook your head a few times as though to clear it, and
lay down on the yellow couch for a nap. This nap became the
dividing point of your life.

I sat on the loveseat and watched you sleep. Your face was
puffy; sweat beaded on your forehead. At the temples little
drops ran down onto the cushions. Your eyelids moved. Darienne came home, looked at you, and went upstairs to practice
while I stayed there watching. You turned sideways and threw
your arm over your cheek. If you were going to get in real trouble now, I thought, then trouble was a consequence of any life
and a step I myself would one day take.

On the couch you slept fitfully, stirring when Darienne
reached the high notes of her scales upstairs. You opened your
eyes, turned halfway toward me, and closed them again. I
picked up a deck of cards from the table between us and practiced shuffling and one-handed cutting. In the early evening
you finally woke, and when you stood and rubbed your eyes and
looked westward into the red horizon, some sort of sense just
clicked on in your head. This was how it happened, I think: you
just decided to change your life. I was standing behind you the
moment I believe you made up your mind. Light still shone
from the west, and you rubbed your eyes and said, "Well."

"Happy birthday," I said.

"Well," you said again, and in the room there actually seemed to be a change in the air. Something went out of it, Lawrence, some force of yours that for my whole life had been charging it like a rainstorm. I turned on the table lamp, came forward, and stood next to you. The smell of liquor and sleep emanated from your clothes. You reached sideways and laid your hand on my shoulder, your heavy, stained fingers lying there with gentleness and intention, and we looked through the window like that until it became dark outside.

Two days later, a Friday, you began fixing up the basement. You came home with a truckload of two-by-fours and plywood sheets in the morning, and by Sunday afternoon you were painting an undercoat on your new apartment. You moved the guest bed up to our old room and moved your own down there, the head against the wall to catch the low light of morning through the single window of clouded glass. We carried down your bureau and the desk we had shared upstairs and the small desk lamp you had won years before in a high school math competition. That night you slept there. Within a couple of weeks you had hung a row of wooden planter boxes along the small outer staircase and planted tulips, our mother's favorite flower. You installed a heater in the corner of the room, hung two fans from the ceiling, and laid down carpet. It was white shag, bought somewhere cheap, and on one corner of it you set up your weight rack and began lifting barbells every morning with the door open and the low eastern sun glinting on the iron.

This was the way you lived the year you changed your life. You didn't go out at night anymore. In the beginning, the phone rang for you five or six times an evening, and when I said that you were busy at the moment, the toneless voices paused, as if considering some knowledge the callers believed I had, then hung up. You had asked me only to take messages. I wrote down who called: Lisa, Marie-Claire, Vicki; your friend Paul

Farmer, the thick-necked bully from Corinth, and John Corsetti, who called you from jail; a group of girls who never left their names. Soon the calls came only two or three times an evening. Then one or two, and finally the phone stopped ringing for you altogether. In May, you enrolled in evening engineering courses at Hill Oak College. Every night after you came home from school, you sat below our living room, the light from your window shining on the cement walkway in the side yard until eleven or twelve o'clock, when you put down your books and did sit-ups and push-ups in the dark before you went to bed. In June, you graduated from St. Vitus, but you kept up your night classes at the college. That summer you took a job at the Chrysler dealership at the highway, first as a mechanic and within a couple of months as supervisor of the mechanics.

Above you in the kitchen, meanwhile, Darienne was painting. She was experimenting with light, and she and our mother would sit at the window and note the multitude of colors that bloomed and faded in the sky above them. She was practicing oboe as well, and when she wasn't doing that she was reading. We were all reading in those days. When we set down our books — Darienne's *Art Through the Ages* or her romance series with raspberry-colored jackets; our mother's small Bibles; my own *World of Insects* or *The Baseball Life of Sandy Koufax* — when we set these down to walk into the living room, we knew that you heard our steps. This knowledge brewed in our minds, and it seemed that our mother was calm because what she had once hoped for, and then given up, she was now hoping for again.

Was it possible for someone to change the way you had? I believed that it was not; but later, as the days grew shorter through the fall and the evening air took on the copper-tasting chill of winter, you didn't waver from the path you had found. Your engineering texts lay open on the desk below your window, and I looked with amazement on the new ideas you were suddenly discovering. On graph paper you drew inclines on which penciled-in balls, and later cars, rolled; you sketched fulcrums and points of balance; you filled pages with circles, lines, and slashes that represented electric circuits. You were learning calculus, a subject that, like physics, was held in front of us lower-school students as something very few people ever, ever understood.

Upstairs, our mother's voice slowly lost the turned-up pitch that had inflected it during the worst months of your adventures. Soon, the Bibles went back on the shelf, where they stayed for a week or two at a time while she and Mrs. Silver read scenes out loud from *Death of a Salesman* instead. Or, rather than read in the afternoons, they walked, and in the evenings they played backgammon on the porch. My beetle collection grew dusty, and I learned to fish instead, which I did smoking a cigarette. I tried to learn to like beer that summer, but never could, and in the fall of the year your life changed, I finally moved across the street to St. Vitus Junior High, where my own days were going to begin in earnest.

Meanwhile, in record time, you earned a degree from Hill Oak College, and Mr. Howland offered you a job. It may have been a favor to our mother or it may have been the part of Mr. Howland's character that drew him to the children he had once reviled. One evening at dinner you announced that St. Vitus had hired you to teach science, whereupon our mother stood up at the table, touched her heart, and said, "We have passed through the night at last."

2

YOU WERE A NEW PERSON in those days — a man, as our mother liked to say, who had turned the corner. You didn't stay out all night anymore; you didn't fight; you didn't wake at Animal's Castle in the early morning, your face pale and your clothes matted with sweat and grass. The next three years passed for me with a serene, happy air that now makes them difficult to recall, as though happiness — contentedness, whatever a child feels — has made them telescope in my memory, the way time itself seemed to be of no great expanse for me in those days. You were the visible prow of our lives, and now you slipped quietly through the world. You read engineering, taught science and car mechanics at St. Vitus, lived in our cellar, and watched my insect collection and Darienne's oil painting with a shrewd, disinterested air that had been the missing element in our lives for a long time.

You had become a docile yet implacable man. In retrospect, I realize that such a demeanor required great strength, and, as I suppose you intended, also reflected it. Once, soon after you began teaching, I was walking with you when a group of toughs from Corinth drove up alongside, threw open the doors of their Pontiac, and swirled onto the sidewalk around us. I had never been in a brawl — I had always been too timid to fight — and I remember the explosion of excitement I felt when, overwhelmed by their number and size, I was ready to get my licks in. I knew we had no chance, but I wheeled and put up my fists. They ignored me. One of them poked you in the chest and squared off, backstepping on the balls of his feet and feinting with his shoulders. You glanced at me, then kept walking: you were a teacher now, you were on your way somewhere. The boy's curved hand darted out and nicked your chin — *slapped* you, really, in the way I knew these fights always started. You stopped and put your hands in your pockets. I stepped up next to you and did the same. The boy approached and feinted a punch to your belly, and you could have done one of two things at that point: you could have stood unflinching, or you could have doubled over to absorb the blow that was coming, for suddenly I knew that you were not going to fight — and what you did was double over, so that when the blow didn't come, when the boy's arm darted back, you were bent forward with your hands still in your pockets, your face toward the sidewalk, while all the boys were laughing. They drove off, hooting at you.

For days after that I tried to imagine what I would have done if they had come at me instead. I would have swung at them, Lawrence, because I was furious at the injustice to you. The humiliation of it burned in me so that I wished over and over that you had not flinched, that you had stood straight so that it would have been the other boy's arm, yanked back in midblow, that would have been laughable, and not you stooped over on the sidewalk. I even began to imagine you had *not* flinched. It was only many years later, as a surgical intern, pausing over the draped, uncut belly of a patient, that I remembered the scene again and understood that you had done the correct thing: your victory was complete. Yours was a reasoned, sure, implacable docility, so carefully thought out it seems now to have been a philosophy, like Gandhi's; it was the *logical* direction for your life.

Why have those years disappeared? Alone with Darienne and our mother upstairs, I moved through that time in surroundings of new quiet that made the world of our family seem suddenly smaller, as though without your troubles it had hushed and shrunk and left me to turn my attention outward. From downstairs the mechanics of your life floated up to us — the morning *clink*, *shffff*, *clink* of your barbells, the knock of your sink pipes, the jingle of your keys each afternoon near five o'clock when you crossed the yard with your suit coat over your shoulder. Your change was a miracle to us, especially to our mother, and the zeal of her religion began to dissipate: you had prompted it and now you had rendered it useless. The Bibles remained in our house but stayed open to the same page for weeks, the red ribbons curling at the ends, the outer column of print fading in the sunlight. Without the Bible on her lap, she sat for hours at a time, looking purposelessly over the porch railing to the yard. Mrs. Silver still sat with her, but in silence, as if they had run out of things to talk about. I know now that she had begun drinking more. In the evenings when she and Mrs. Silver came inside from the porch, her cheeks were flushed and her step was ungraceful on the stairs. Without knowing it, I think, she was disappointed in your change.

But the change seemed genuine: you had become an earnest, helpful citizen. At St. Vitus High, where I was now a freshman, the marginal students gathered around you, and many times I saw you walk among them in the halls, your head partway bowed, shining with the humility of the converted; their own talk quieted and turned to you. On Saturdays you helped Mr. Howland run the Community Club, which many of these troubled students had joined. The Community Club was for these kids especially, the ones who needed to be redeemed. It was the kind of group one no longer sees, at least not in the city where I live. You, the paradigm of redemption, helped Mr. Howland lead it; and I was a member too — mostly, I believe, because I was your brother.

Now, of course, I wonder what made you take part in it. Were you only trying to keep your job? Did Henry Howland insist, or was it you who had wanted to be near him? You drove the second van on our outings, led the repair trips we occasionally made to the old people's home in Chester Bay, and now and then spoke to us about discipline. I was a good student — as you had been — and I had never been in any real sort of trouble, but I never doubted why I was asked to join. I carried in me a clear sense of wrongdoing, and when Mr. Howland called me to his office one morning in May of my first year in high school, I knew what he was going to tell me. I was fifteen and infected with an inexplicable, black doubt. Was it simply *your* past, Lawrence, your wild lurch through life six years ahead of me, that made me think I had done something wrong as well?

At my first club meeting, I remember, each of us had to compile a list of the assets and deficiencies of our characters — the kind of thing we would do all summer during the clubhouse hours. We sat in a basement classroom, while before us, standing at the maple lectern you had built for him, Mr. Howland adjusted and readjusted his bifocals. Down the aisle behind us, in a metal chair separate from the rest, you yourself sat with an unmoving gaze. You had nodded at me when I entered, but that was all. In a tie and button-down collar you sat silently, as you would sit silently at all our meetings from then on, speaking only when you took the podium, and then in a voice we had to lean forward to hear. In those days, you played this part to perfection.

Once or twice on that first day I glanced behind me: the air conditioner was rattling, and as Mr. Howland spoke I watched it drip a slow trickle of greenish water onto the floorboards around your unmoving feet. Your gaze did not waver. I drummed my fingers on my knees. Even in the group of twenty of us, twelve boys and eight girls, your presence made me sure I had been singled out by Mr. Howland. When he pushed down the bifocals on his nose and cast his thick, graying eyebrows in my direction, I didn't know whether it was a gesture of welcome or of disapproval. I looked away.

He was a master at this sort of silent prosecution. The summer before, at our junior high graduation banquet, I had first heard him speak to a crowd. The banquet was held in the basement recreation room, which had been filled with shellacked tables the size of cars. At the end of dinner we heard speeches from our teachers and from one or two unliked students, who read their lines from index cards. Then Mr. Howland, whom I had seen countless times helping our mother with the dishes in our kitchen, stood at the head table on the stage, and I saw him in a way I never had before. He thumped the table once and began to speak. He started with a prayer. Then he reviewed the year for us, our triumphs and misbehaviors, the championship for our baseball team — here his voice rose — and the near championship for the hockey players — here it fell again. He whispered the story of the unfortunate two students, now long gone from the school, who had copied their themes from the Cliff Notes. Then he fell silent. For several seconds he gazed at us. As he stood there, raised above us on the small stage, the room in shadow, I felt even in June that the summer — barely arrived — was already tipping its weight. He began speaking again, in a low voice, about his hopes for us, and as he did so the just perceptible dread of autumn filled me. His low words and the oratorical movement of his hands reminded me of the approach of next year's newly varnished school floors, of the narrow, wood-smelling corridors and the early darkness of fall. He used the old man's trick of narrowing his eyes during silences, a technique he employed in his office to draw out students' confessions. His words hung, heavy and expectant, in our minds, his pauses rooting through our consciences like smoke. He paused and rapped the table. He squinted. As he neared the end of his speech, the large room dark around him, all of us silent while our teachers came up behind us to set down tin bowls filled with halved Cling peaches in syrup, I thought of his daughter. Mr. Howland's sadness, his October chill, his oratorical threats, the embrace of injustice that led him to pick the truants among us as his flock: these things always led me back to Lottie.

Now, in my first meeting of the Community Club, I listed my character deficiencies: I was irreligious; I cared too much about myself and not enough about others; I was lazy. And I was envious — of Darienne, for example, and her easy entrance into our mother's and Mrs. Silver's lives; and of you, for the clear, forward path you struck through the world — I truly envied that, Lawrence. I also noted that on a few occasions I had stolen, and that I had had lewd thoughts. But all these were a distraction so that I could avoid writing down what I suspected was my most serious flaw of all, the one that had probably brought me here: in my heart, I knew that everything you had done in your wild past I could as easily have done myself.

Standing at the front of the room, Mr. Howland pushed down his glasses again. Behind me I could hear your steady breathing — even when I couldn't see you, Lawrence, I could always discern your presence. I stared at my paper. *Can't dedicate myself to anything*, I wrote. *Unsympathetic to people*, and at that moment the whirr of Lottie Howland's wheelchair came to us from outside. Years later I realized that Mr. Howland had probably staged this small scene, as a lesson. That was the way he was. We heard the gears change as she rolled down the outside ramp to the basement, the squeal of rubber rims on our varnished floor, a shift again, and the penetrating, forward-moving sound of her chair. The door to the classroom opened and she moved across the room in front of her father; he leaned down to listen to her. I was always embarrassed to see Lottie, if only because of the evenings she had spent at our house, her legs covered by a dark blanket and her head bobbing as she ate. Now I looked at the metal braces on her ankles. More than anything else about her these braces drew my eye, their black, straight run from above her skirt hem down her thighs to the soles of her feet, where there was a joint and they bent under. This bend, this flat, short width of metal that ran underneath the arch of her foot — there was something about it, Lawrence, I didn't know what: I closed my eyes.

When I opened them he had laid his hand on her shoulder. She looked up quickly, her hair falling in dry ringlets across the rubber-coated handles by her arms. The bounce of that hair gripped me. It was washed and shiny and full of light; on another girl it would have been beautiful. Her mouth was full as well, but it lacked motion, and at its corner she had tucked the flesh-colored cord of her hearing aid. She stayed only a moment: she whispered to her father, nodded at all of us seated silently before her, and left.

Mr. Howland held the door long after she had moved into the hall. Then he looked back at us over the tops of his glasses: here was a man, we knew, who had been sorely tried by God. That he had a crippled daughter and a wife who had passed away was always present in his face, in its dark lines, in the righteous, accusatory look he always wore. We understood from this look that his faith should be a beacon to us; it had been tested the way none of ours had.

And his kindnesses — though he was a disciplinarian by nature, he could convey the trustworthy gentleness of a priest — his kindnesses were often deep and surprising. I wonder whether you ever saw this part of him, Lawrence. In school, for instance, he visited anybody who had been sent to the infirmary: he liked to rest his thick hands on our shoulders as we lay in the nurse's single cot by the window, and such gentle concern gave to the general harshness of his discipline the added crime of our having disappointed a kind man. And of course our mother always insisted that he was unfailingly kind and generous, despite his trials. Only you, who were now his disciple, had disagreed.

He had stopped speaking and was scrutinizing us again. I looked down at my paper. For virtues, I wrote *Good Student, Friendly, Well informed*. I was well informed because of you, Lawrence: I knew that fish bit before a rain, that aluminum corroded copper, that weather came from the west. Mr. Howland gazed at us over his bifocals, arching his gray, kinetic eyebrows, his loose cheeks puffing with his breaths. It seemed that every time I glanced up from my writing he was concentrating on me.

Indeed, at the end of our meeting that first day he asked to speak with me: after lunch I walked around the short yard at his side and entered the building through the side door. It swung shut, and I could see almost nothing until he reached to the wall and the light snapped on. What did he want? I wonder whether he did, in fact, bear a special animosity toward you, Lawrence; perhaps this carried over to his feelings for me. We were in a long hallway faced with brick and cut by square columns in which the workings of the building ran.

"Well, well," he said.

I smiled at him.

"I know your brother better than I know you, but I'm glad I have the chance to learn about you a little earlier."

"So am I."

He pushed up his glasses and ran his finger across the bridge of his nose. "I want us to understand each other, though. Do we, Edward Sellers?"

I looked at him.

"That's important," he said. "That's got to be clear."

"I guess so," I said. I did not understand, and all I can imagine now is that he, in innocence, was merely trying to divert me from the road he had watched you take.

He stood in front of me with his hands on his waist. "Your brother had some odd ideas about himself, but I can see that you don't have them." He raised his eyebrows and I looked down. "Do you know what I mean?"

"Not exactly."

"Your brother thought he was more important than he was," he said. "That's what happened to him. Is that going to happen to you?" He stood motionless, his big hands resting on the sideward protrusion of his hips, and only at that moment, in the reflection of the swinging glass door at the end of the corridor, did I notice you behind me.

"Pardon?" I said.

I turned around and glanced at you, standing there with your head lowered and your hands in your pockets. You were a teacher, Lawrence. What in God's name were you thinking in those days? Mr. Howland didn't look at you, but he moved his chin in your direction. "He seems unimportant to you right now," he said, "but that's not right." He rubbed his brow. "Important and unimportant don't matter, really. He's humble now, and that's what matters." He nodded at you without looking, a habit he would maintain all that summer. I glanced around at you again, and though you still had your head down, I could see your restrained expression. Mr. Howland thought it was the look of humility, but even then I should have known it was not; it was a *resolved* look, and you had been wearing it for years.

"You can be important and still be humble," Mr. Howland said. "That's what matters — right?"

"Yes, sir."

"You don't know what I'm talking about, do you?"

"Yes, I do."

"No, you don't. It has to do with accepting the Lord's power." He narrowed his eyes. "How can you know anything about that?"

"I can."

"Of course you cannot," he said, and when I looked up he was smiling. He nodded in your direction again. "But Lawrence understands that, and one day you will, too." He looked at me gravely. "Shake," he said.

I extended my hand. He took it, then reached out and pulled my other one sharply out of its sleeve and held them both in front of him. In the buzzing light of the ceiling bulb he turned them over once, then again, his rough fingers pressing into my palms. I knew what he was looking for, Lawrence, and it was a failing of mine that I felt not anger but shame: for this I apologize. He smelled of hair tonic. At last he put down my hands and looked into my eyes. His own were veined and yellowish, and I stood for several moments looking into them, not saying anything, while the ceiling light hummed above us and you stood to the side, as still as an apparition.

That was how the summer began. It was late June: the humid air had descended, the farmers' full fields no longer rustled in the breezes, and at the bluff the sweet smell of riverweeds rose from the banks. At home, Mrs. Silver and our mother were reading *The Bridge of San Luis Rey* outside in the afternoons, standing at the porch rail for the long orations, looking out over our yard where the grass lay limp with heat. You spent your time in the apartment downstairs. Upstairs in her room, where the carpet muted the sound but could not hide it, Darienne was memorizing the Bellini oboe concerto for her concert in August with the county high school orchestra. She was painting, too, and in her earnest way, wrapped in her queer awe, she was memorizing "Kubla Khan," by Samuel Taylor Coleridge. Our sister lived in a different world. She had written out the verses and taped them next to the mirror in our bathroom. " 'In Xanadu did Kubla Khan,' " I absently read each morning as I combed my hair, " 'A stately pleasure dome decree.' "

" 'Where Alph, the sacred river, ran,' " she would mumble at breakfast while I ate Rice Chex and read the baseball scores. " 'Through caverns measureless to man, Down to a sunless sea.' " She would pause and gesture between us with her hand. " 'Through caverns *measureless to man*,' " she would repeat, and pause, and gesture again in front of the cereal box before she lowered her voice dramatically. " 'Down to a sunless sea.' "

"Milk please, Dary."

I myself was not devoted to anything the way you and Darienne were. You reading, Darienne memorizing, the world seemed to recede from you both. But for me it was there every moment, hot and beckoning, so that I often had the sense I was in the wrong place and was missing something. Nothing in particular interested me, but everything in my life was turned up a pitch by the heat. As a show of discipline and an acknowledgment of the way you two parceled out your dedications, I had kept up my insect collecting, but for months at a time I was bored with it. There was just one insect I truly wanted to find, a beetle so rare only a handful had been pinned, though I knew in my heart that I wanted it not for the scientific satisfaction but to please you: Lawrence, that was all I wanted. It was called Yellow Nightshine, and in *World of Insects* it lay across its own half-page print. Its coleopteric armor shone with a metallic yellow so brilliant the hue itself created a yearning in me that I felt in my throat, like thirst. I looked for it in tree trunks; I looked in the worm-eaten decay of driftwood and under plate-sized slabs of stone that I dug out and lifted; in the cool woods and steaming fields I walked bent forward, searching. I suspected — I *knew*, really, because at that age I had not yet felt a real disappointment — I knew that I would one day find it. From behind stumps, from under trees, from along the gray-green undersides of leaves I waited for the wobble of its eerie, iron-red leg stripes and the sun-yellow metal of its armor.

Otherwise, I collected only in occasional fits that began with my dusting off the rows of cork mounts on the shaded shelf below my window. My collection was slowly growing. On the wall of my room stood a chart of the phylum Arthropoda and the class Insecta. I went collecting in the farmers' lands south of town, scooping what I caught into the killing jar you had given me. It was scribed with measure marks and inset with a magnifying lens. I trapped the yellow-winged corn borer; with my net I swept the bobbing waterlilies for leaf beatles; from under rotting bark I routed scrambling troops of weevils. At home I dried and mounted them and set them on a wide cork plate on which I one day hoped to catalogue the order Coleoptera.

Lying in my bed I absently absorbed morphology from the chart on my wall. My eyes lingered on the intricate line render-

ings of mayflies and springtails, on the overweight proboscises
of the Lepidoptera, on the firebrat's nightmarish, groping tail.
Each order was appointed with a finely rendered plan of the
body, leg, and wing. I held our magnifying lens over each new
find. I had dung beetles and net-winged beetles, tiny carpet beetles, a ground beetle as long as my pinky, a fur-legged checkered
beetle I bought from an entomologist's supply house in Vir-
ginia. For weeks I would lose interest in the rows of tiny hardened shells at the back of my work table, but soon the
miniature leg bristles, the near-hairy perfection of them, would
touch a crazy longing in me, and I would dust everything,
mount a new row, and relabel the flat slices of cork. I would go
out into the woods on a Saturday at dawn, sift through mounds
of compost for Yellow Nightshine while the cold dew turned
the scrambles of all the ordinary beetles into sluggardly walks
and made them oddly unafraid of my tiny net.

Those beetles were my only tie to devotion, I sometimes
think, the remnant in me of what you and our sister and
mother felt but that I did not. I knew only vague desires and
elusive longings, and I was dogged with the sense that I indeed
had missed something. Perhaps devotion was it. Perhaps that
was the family gene that had passed me over. You, after all,
though you forswore faith, had your own religion: you studied
it with an atheist's passion.

Meanwhile, in the damp woods and the still fields, at the
bluff above the bubbling river and in the dark meeting hall of
the Community Club, I searched for my own. Mr. Howland
told us we would find it through sacrifice, and sacrifice was the
idea he stressed at our meetings. We sat in large groups, then in
smaller groups, then alone, thinking of ways to give ourselves
to the town of Blue River. We planted flowers, swept the streets
clean of garbage, built a low wooden fence along the palisade

where the primary school students sat in the afternoons. We met twice a week. Tuesday evenings the meetings took place in the club lounge at the Hotel Mississippi, a room that was bare except for our twenty folding chairs and the map of Wisconsin on which a red-topped pin had been buried over Blue River; on Saturday mornings we met in the basement of the church, and for two hours after those meetings we did our errands. Most of them were labors of kindness for old people. We walked them to doctors' appointments or carried in crates of canned foods to their dusty pantries. More than once we moved their beds when they died.

One of the first errands of mercy we did was for Keris Salmon, whose house had caught fire early in the summer, one June night when sheets of heat lightning were exploding like flashbulbs along the horizon. The house was small and nearly engulfed by the time the fire engines arrived; we heard that Keris — a dark-browed, serious man now, no longer the boy who had tricked you into skinny dipping — had stood weeping on the lawn as his house collapsed, room by room, before him. The next day the Community Club sifted through the burned shell with him, depositing everything we found — keys, silverware, scissors, all the metal possessions of his life, turned black by the heat and the firehoses — into buckets of soapwater that frothed over with the ashes. He thanked us profusely, and cried again when we handed him the things we had found: a stapler, some forks, a trowel.

The summer had already set a record for fires. June had been unusually hot, the air rippling with heat lightning and the sky rimmed with haze. The roads were soft. Before the Salmons', two houses had already burned in Corinth. Both fires happened at night, both infernos that raged along the bluff and lit the sky and river. We had all gone out to watch them, standing with

Mr. Howland on the upwind cliffs and waiting for the rafters to crumble and the spark showers to rocket into the sky.

The mornings after the fires, the Community Club met early, on the lawn of the church, and we walked together down the cutback stairs to the river. There, Mr. Howland spoke to us with the newly risen sun behind him. He took advantage of these days. Gathered on the cool beach before him, we trembled with the proximity of important events, and at the river the silence of the dawn seemed to deepen: I could hear the slipping rollover of currents, the wallop of surface fish breaching at midriver, the distant thrum of grasshoppers. Death and life were all around us, and the clouds cast their pale reflections on the water. Nobody whispered on these mornings, nobody laughed; each of us was quiet with the sense of wonder that even then we had. Here, I suspected, was where faith would one day come to me, the way Jesus came to men on journeys. Mr. Howland knew this, I believe — he had the preacher in him; he knew that a rising sun or a morning vista of dewy grass gave his words a melancholy solemnity, a sense of both hope and fate that made even a small pronouncement seem a crux in our lives. But the things he talked to us about, standing on the summit of a farmer's low hill or on a rock a half dozen feet in the river, the things he told us on those days — little things like, "You are going to have responsibility to other people soon," or, "The fall of one of you is the beginning of the demise of you all" — these things filled me not just with solemnity or burden, as I suppose he intended, but with eagerness; as if now, at last, we could get on with our lives. He lowered his voice, and for the rest of the day I found mine lowered as well. I felt all around me the imminence of change.

By the time the heat peaked that summer, I had become friends with a boy in the Community Club named Zoltan Morris. Zoltan was new in Blue River; he had no other friends and probably would not have made any, although alone with me he spoke with a mean conviction. His eyes were narrow; his nose was flattened like a boxer's. Did I know his future, as you would later suggest? He was harsh and condemnatory and fat, but there was something to his harshness that was irresistible: he, like you, was sure of things.

He always stood with his hands in his pockets. "Grab one for me, Zoltan," the other boys would say, shuffling past him in the corridor of the church basement, their heads turned the other way. I had first gone to his house in June, when his mother invited me over, and from the start I felt drawn to him. A small white desk stood by the window in his room, with a small white chair pushed in against it; on the walls hung some pennants and a collection of baseball gloves from an earlier era, with leather fingers that were not lashed together, though Zoltan himself was a dismal athlete. That afternoon, he paced his room; then he sat down on the windowsill and looked away from me into their birch.

"You're the only one in that whole club who's worth it," he said.

"Worth what?"

"Worth the time of day, Sellers."

"Well, thanks, Morris — I guess."

He put his hands in his pockets. Still looking into the tree, he began working his fingers. "And that's why I'm going to let you in on a little secret."

I laughed. "Is it a secret I want to know?"

"Get this, Sellers," he said. "Zoltan Morris only has one ball."

"What?"

"I only have one testicle, man. The other one never came down."

I laughed again. "Came down from where?"

"That's how you get them. They come down from inside." He turned and brushed his hand across his belly. "Mine never came down."

"Jeez."

"You're the only person who knows." His eyes were touched with regret now.

"I won't tell anybody."

He spit into his wastebasket. "Shit," he said, "You will too."

"What do you mean?"

"I know you will."

"Then why'd you tell me?"

"I wanted to see if I could trust you."

"Trust *me*?" I said. I pointed at my chest. "You can trust me."

Lawrence, he was so similar to you in this. Why did he want to test my fidelity? Why did you later want the same? He walked away from the window and stood facing the wall.

"I told my mother we were friends," he said.

"What'd she say?"

He lit a match and tossed it into the basket, where it smoked but didn't ignite. "Nothing," he said. "She doesn't give a damn."

"All right," I said. "We're friends."

So after that we tried to be. What was it that drew me to him, I wonder — a perverse, secret boy with the air of an eavesdropper, a boy who exhibited his self-loathing as a weapon? Why did I spend that summer with him? Over the next weeks, we began passing our days together. We were at an interesting age: it may be true that we hated each other. We went fishing Sunday mornings right after church, and as we walked out on the rock pier to where the river bottom dropped off and hid the two-pound bass, I sometimes wished he would slip off into the water. He, I knew, wished the same for me. A yellowish moss grew on the rocks and made the possibility real. Walking ahead of him, I tried to look particularly at ease; walking behind, I hurried so that he would have to do the same. I knew he wasn't much of a swimmer; once, on a Community Club outing, he had jumped into the pool and sunk to the bottom like a packed suitcase; Mr. Howland had to dive in to pull him out, and though Zoltan was under for only a few seconds, he emerged coughing and unable to stand on his own for several minutes. After that day, some of the boys stopped teasing him.

But when we fished together, we nonetheless sat on the farthest rocks of the pier. We cast our spinners into the current that frothed in turmoil around us. This far out, the river's oceanic strength produced a low murmur like an engine. We listened to that murmur, sat watching our lines dip and resurface downstream, and tried to discern the pull of water from the mouth suck of a bass. Whole trees floated by, and the wind sometimes made the top current flow backward.

One day just beyond the reach of our lines a sunken motorboat drifted past. It dipped downriver while we sat there, its bridge canopy barely breaking the surface; below, the submerged hull angled away from us like the shadow of a shark. We reeled in our lines and cast toward it, our lead shot plinking into the waves a dozen yards short of the breaching canopy. I'm not sure what we were trying to do; we obviously could not stop it. I thought of the owners. Were they inside, their lungs filled with muddy water? Dread entered my gut. When I thought of motorboats, I thought of the blond girls in striped bikinis at the Belaire resort, girls who wore sunglasses dangling from their necks and drank sweating white cans of Fresca on the decks while underneath them the boats made gurgling, gas-pocked noises and stood still, the hulls squeaking against the dock. Was there such a girl inside, the current moving over her? As it passed beyond us, the boat caught and pivoted. The river welled up behind and pushed; in front, it was sucked down into a vortex. I was fascinated. It was not just dread I felt, Lawrence, even if inside sat a family, brown water streaming through their hair; it was also excitement. I wanted to see them. The boat dipped below again and disappeared, and we didn't spot it until the canopy resurfaced twenty yards downriver and headed away from us. I cast my line.

"Wow," Zoltan whispered.

We stood there, swallowed in our thoughts of the river. While my spinner floated at its downstream angle, I kept my finger on the line. Everything was being transmitted to me — the buzz in the pockets of quick current, the gentle stroke of weed tips, the hummingbird's pull of the whirling, streamlined blades. The spinner plocked against hidden bodies, moved around them, slid on through the brown river. I imagined the big, secret bass, hidden somewhere in the deep water, waiting us out, their noses turned upriver in the shade of weeds, their dark eyes following the twirling silver blink of our lures.

"You see how they say that," you said the next afternoon, " 'the flock'?" You picked at your tooth. "You want to be part of that? 'The flock'? You think that's an honor, to be one of a herd of sheep?"

"No," I said. We were in your apartment, and you were reading out loud from *The Light*, our mother's magazine. I looked at you. When I recall that summer, I believe this may have been the first moment I understood something was about to go badly wrong.

"That's why I've taught you all this, Ed. That's what science did. It freed people from this stuff."

"I like biology."

You put down the magazine. "Here's a question for you. Think about it, though, and when you have an idea, try me." You placed your hands flat in front of you on the desk.

"What's the question?"

"The question is: What was the most important discovery of all time?"

"The wheel."

"Don't be stupid."

"What's stupid about that?"

"It's stupid because it's just something you've heard. Think about things, Ed."

"I do."

"No, you don't."

That evening at dinner I asked Darienne. She thought for several minutes, gazing dreamily up at the kitchen ceiling. "Perspective," she finally said. She nodded at us. "Brunelleschi."

"Who?"

"Before Brunelleschi," she said, "painters only had atmosphere to make depth." She stood up and gestured out the low window of the kitchen toward the river. Mrs. Silver put down her spoon and looked through the glass. It was ninety degrees outside and our mother had made cold tomato soup. "They used clouds to show distance, they made things blurry that were far away." She walked back toward us. You stirred your bowl and watched her. She was unaccustomed to your attention and was drawing out her words. "Finally," she said, reaching one hand into the air, "Brunelleschi figured out the vanishing point."

She stood in front of us, regarding her hand in the air.

"Hah!" I said.

"Go to the devil, Edward."

"Darienne," said our mother.

"Sorry."

"Wait a minute," you said slowly. "You're saying that that's the most important discovery of all time?" You looked at your soup. "You're saying the vanishing point at the top of a canvas is the most important creation ever? That's not important, Dary. That's *idiotic*."

Our mother looked up, alarmed. "It certainly seems important to me," she said.

"To me, too," said Darienne. She let her raised hand fall to her side. "It's the *most* important to me."

"Wait a second, Dary," I said. "What about the electric light? Try painting at night without that one. And what about fire? What about a combustion engine? What about penicillin?"

"I don't care about any of those."

I looked at you. On your face was the remote expression you used to dismiss people. You picked up your bowl and drank from it.

Our mother was studying you. "You know what *I* think is the most important invention of all time?" she said.

"What?" said Darienne.

"Skepticism."

We all looked at her. She smiled beatifically at you, and you half-smiled back. "Because without it," she said, "faith would have no value." She sighed gently.

Nobody said anything. You put down your bowl, picked up your soup spoon, and dipped it. Our mother still looked at you. You swallowed a mouthful and she kept looking.

"Good soup," said Darienne.

"Thank you, Darienne."

"Yeah," I said.

"Thank you, Edward."

I ate a spoonful and smiled at our mother. "Mrs. Silver," I said, "what do *you* think is the most important invention of all time?"

She thought for a moment. "Air conditioning," she said.

The next day I asked Zoltan. We were in his room. "What are you talking about, Sellers?"

"It's a question, that's all. What do you think is the most important thing anyone's ever invented?"

"Ben wah balls," he said.

"What?"

"Ben wah balls."

"Maybe."

"You don't even know what they are."

"That's right," I said. "I don't."

He went to his desk, reached into the drawer, and pulled out two shiny metal balls the size of shooter marbles.

"Voilà," he said. He held them up between his thumb and forefinger. "Ben wah balls."

"Big deal."

He lowered his hands to his zipper. "Girls use them," he said. He rubbed his thighs together. "They put them inside." He smiled.

For several days, I thought about inventions. Without fire, I reasoned, there would have been little use for the wheel, but without the wheel cities could not have been built. On the other hand, Gutenberg's printing press or the motto we had learned of the French Revolution — *liberté, égalité, fraternité* — might have been the kind of unlikely answer you would think of. Penicillin seemed important, as did anaesthesia and the steam engine.

"Okay," I said to you the next evening. "I have an idea."

You were reading *The Skeptic*. "The answer is the scientific method," you said.

"You didn't even let me try."

"You wouldn't have gotten it."

"How do you know?"

"I just do."

"Jeez, Lawrence."

"Well, would you have gotten it?"

"No."

"Okay then."

I went to the window. "The scientific method was an invention?"

"It sure was," you said. "It's the one that made all the others possible."

A thunderstorm was moving toward us from across the river. "Well," I said, "that's a disappointment."

"Next time I'll tell you something more interesting." You smiled, picked up your copy of *The Skeptic*, and went on reading.

The next morning I approached Darienne, standing on newspapers on the living room floor, painting. "I think the scientific method is the most important invention of all time," I said.

"Where'd you get that idea?"

"I was just thinking about it."

"Well, I don't agree."

"You don't even know what it is."

She sighted out the window with her thumb. I saw that she was trying to paint the difference between what she saw through the bottom pane, which was open, and the top, which was closed. "Well," she said, "that proves it's not important."

I stood behind her. "The nasturtiums are yellower than that," I said.

Her hand stopped and she looked out the window; then she

touched the brush to the canvas again. The colors above the sash were whitened, which gave them a sheen that suggested glass. "I'm eighteen," she said, without looking up. "I'll be gone soon and you'll never have known me." She put down the brush. "Isn't *that* important to you?"

"Of course, Dary." I sat on the windowsill. "Where are you planning to go?"

"That's not my point. The point is that *I* run this family, and soon I won't be able to."

"*You* run it?"

"Yes."

"Hah!" I said. "Lawrence does."

"He does not, dummy." She twirled the brush in the thinner. "He does things so he can pretend to, like that business" — she paused — "like that business with the most important discovery. But I'm the one who holds us together."

"Dary, I just don't think perspective can be the most important discovery in history."

"I'm not saying it is."

"Okay," I said, "fine." I leaned over to examine her work. She touched yellow to the heads of the nasturtiums. "Without me here," she said, "Lawrence would have torn you apart."

"Torn *me* apart?"

"That's right."

She tilted her head toward the canvas, and I looked down into the cowlick of her hair. "I'm sorry, Dary." I said. "I'm obliged to look at this scientifically, and I just don't see it."

One Saturday morning in the Community Club, while we were supposed to be imagining new forms of service to Blue River, I leaned toward Zoltan and pointed to Anita Candle, a girl I had known all my life. "I'm in love with her," I whispered.

He had been cleaning his fingernails. "Who?"

"Her."

He craned his neck to look. "Spare me," he whispered.

Anita had straight brown hair, heavy lids over her nearly black eyes, and a frankness to all her gestures that I could see even from here, two rows behind the back of her metal chair. We had kissed that spring and summer on our back porch. Those long afternoons had put her perfume into my shirts, and now I could smell it again. Trapped wasps — crazed, like me, with the odors — had batted the top corners of the screens.

Zoltan leaned forward. "Anita Candle?" he whispered. "It's hopeless, Edward."

"No, it's not."

"She's the Queen of France."

"The what?"

"The Queen of France. Marie Antoinette." He drew his hand across his throat. "Plop."

I lowered my voice. "We've done a lot, Zoltan."

"You?"

"Yeah."

"Hah!" he barked; in front of us, Mr. Howland raised his head from his book.

I looked away, pretended to think, then pretended to write something down. Mr. Howland went back to reading.

Next to me, Zoltan laughed again. "You have not. You're a fatso, Sellers; she's the Queen."

I scowled at him. He was the fat one, and he had a fake front tooth that made the other ones look yellow. I wanted to hit him. He had a rare quality, a mean but pathetic strength; it showed in his smile, which was wide-lipped and sarcastic and appeared below his narrow, shamed eyes that were like pebbles.

He was an awkward slob, and although Anita was not what many boys considered beautiful, she possessed a confidence in her stride and speech that made her seem older than the rest of us. Zoltan worked his jaw. "She's the Queen, all right," he said, "and you're the peasant."

That afternoon we walked to his house. I was sullen, though I would never have said so: I walked behind him, tossing stones over the embankment and slowing my stride so that he had to stop until I caught up with him. At his house, we went out the back door into the grassless yard, and from there down a small slope to a path that ran through the tangles of thornbushes between their property and the small woods behind it. He wanted to show me something. Most of the trees had been cut here, and the saplings and undergrowth intruded. The path was narrow and he walked ahead of me, panting. "I'm sorry what I said about you and Anita," he finally said. Like many sad boys, he was old beyond his years.

"That's all right," I said. I was no longer angry. "She *is* sort of queenish. What are you going to show me?"

"Patience, Sellers. Patience."

We kept walking, down the gentle slope of the path into the older, widely spaced stands of birch where the undergrowth thinned out. He tried to whistle but didn't have enough breath. Soon we came upon a tiny logger's shed. It was big enough for one man's tools, a small chair, and little else; its slanted roof was barely taller than my head. The brush had been removed around it, and a small clearing, six or seven feet wide, allowed the sun to intrude.

"What do you think?" he said, resting forward with his hands on his knees.

"It's a logger's shed. They're all over."

"I cleared the land around it."

"They all leak. We used to hide in them."

"So?"

"So, is that all you wanted to show me, a logger's shed?"

He stood up. "There's more. Stand there," he said, pointing to the edge of the clearing, "and watch this."

He disappeared into the side door and I walked to the edge of the woods and stood against a tree. "Yeah?"

"Keep watching."

"I am, Zoltan." He was moving something around inside. "Are you still watching?"

"Sure am."

"Who's the Queen of France?" he called.

"Anita Candle."

"Who do we love?"

"Anita Candle."

"Okay," he said. He ducked out the entrance, moved quickly across the clearing, and sat on the ground in front of me.

"So?"

There was a sound like a fan turning on, and suddenly the shed was engulfed in flames. They pitched out from the small window and the open door and in an instant shot through the roof and blazed up twenty feet, licking for a few seconds among the green, outermost branches of the trees, snapping with the sound of whips, before they receded again. "Mother!" I whispered. "You're crazy." He smiled his yellow teeth at me. The fire began moving inside in crackling bursts, rising when it met new wood, running steadily through the thinly framed walls. In a few minutes the whole structure would be gone. I stepped into the clearing, where Zoltan took hold of my shoulder. "You going to pee on it?"

"You're going to kill yourself, Zoltan."

"Take it easy, Casanova."

"You're going to burn the whole damn forest."

He shook his head. "That's why I cleared it."

I sat down. The gray smoke had risen and formed a cloud above us that thickened in the still air and began to dim the sunlight. The fire had calmed now, and I watched it complete its move up the low walls. None of the trees had caught. Their leaves shifted in the breeze that moved outward from the clearing. Presently a side wall caved in, and after a few more minutes the front, and soon the whole shed had fallen in on itself so that after a time it burned like a fire in a hearth, the lumber crossed in a pile, flaming and breaking and crackling as it settled toward the ground. We sat without speaking, Zoltan's nostrils flaring open to take in the smoky air. Nobody I had ever known seemed crazy, but as I sat there next to him, breathing through my cotton shirtsleeve, that was what I thought Zoltan was. Still, though, there was something about him — I didn't know what — something about him that kept me with him. He coughed and pinched his nose. His face was red. I got up and sauntered over to the pile of burned timber, which I moved around with a stick, breaking it up so that the new wood caught. I stamped the embers into the ground with my heels. "How'd you do that?" I said finally.

He moved his hand in his pocket. "Tricks," he said.

After that, through the middle days of summer when the heat gathered daily in the air and haze hid the stars at night, when each morning was warmer than the last and the after-noons thickened like liquid, we burned things. We burned trash in his basement and driftwood at night along the shore, and another logger's shed one afternoon after we had cleared the brush around it with a sickle he had found in a field. I don't know why we did this: we were kids. One night we nailed boards into a platform that we filled with doused newspaper, kindling sticks, and firecrackers, and launched into the river with a pack of burning Ohio Blue Tips; the shaky contraption floated away at the shallow angle of the rift, dipping in the current, smoking profusely but flaming only in tiny licks until it reached the wind at the deep water; there, it burst into a conflagration, erupting with explosions as we pounded each other's back and watched it drift into the dark like a beacon. The next night we burned a dock.

Then I got scared. This is when I told you about it, Lawrence. "Zoltan's burning things," I said to you one morning in your room; "big things." And though I was burning them with him, it seemed to me that I was nonetheless telling you the truth — that I was only the accomplice in all of this, just as I had always been, in a way, nothing more than the accomplice in your own affairs.

"Be careful," you said. "That kid's bad news." You went to the window and looked up into the light of the yard. I moved next to you. "He's not going to stop," you said. "You know that? He's not the kind who can."

I wonder now, Lawrence, how much of the future you had envisioned at that moment as we stood together at your window and looked up into the yard, where across the grass the oak leaves hung limply in the heat and in the distance the concrete spire of St. Vitus stood in the haze like the gray cone of a rocket. "Amazing," you said. "The kid's a real arsonist."

Zoltan's house stood at the end of the path that ran parallel to Edge Road, a few hundred feet from the triangular point of land where the bluff dipped closest to the water, and from his back yard a path led down the short cliff to a narrow stretch of bank that ran south, appearing and disappearing, toward where we lived. After heavy rain the shore was gone completely, but the coves and small bends always presented a path of shallow water; here, Zoltan explored the river. Next to the old baseball

gloves on his wall he had hung his waterlogged finds: a fishing
pole, dozens of chipped lures, oars, a boat radio, a polystyrene
life ring, and an old-fashioned, algae-blackened wooden water
ski on which the name *Dottie Gerrity* had been burned into the
shellac. He had a lady's purse, with lipstick containers, a mirror, and a darkened five-dollar bill hung next to it.

One Saturday morning he led me down the hill to the water
and we went south, not the way we usually went, farther away
from town along the sweeping curve of bank where shrubs and
grasses grew and the bluff tapered off to a gradual hill. The
water was slow here and the banks gave off the sweet smell of
river mud. As we walked the shoreline, our sneakers pulled at
the shiny coat of riverweed. He had something new to show
me, he said. The sun was still low in the sky, and shadow covered the eastern half of the river. Out in the rift, sunning carp
bumped the still surface; at this hour the oily water showed
every ripple where their brown backs broke through. As we approached a bend, he slowed down, crouched forward, and made
his way to a stand of leafless bushes that stood ankle-deep in
the silty water. When I came up behind him he motioned for
me to keep still, and together we crouched behind the brittle,
silt-killed shrubs and peered around the bend to the narrow
beach. I saw rocks, a narrow spit of dark sand, and the wide,
uncovered mud below the high-water mark. Above the beach
the hill led back to a line of low trees and disappeared.

"What are we looking at?"

"Shhh."

"I don't see anything, Zoltan."

"We're early."

"Early for what?"

"Shhh."

The air was already hot, and I sat down in my shorts in the
shallow current. I leaned back, closed my eyes, and rested my

head in the warm water; the buzzes and small clicks of the river filled my ears. Above us the sun climbed, lighting up my eyelids until they swam with color. An arm's length to the right of us, the bottom dropped off and the river's earnest torrent began. I listened to its hums.

"Okay, Sellers," Zoltan said quietly. "I told you."

When I sat up, it took me several seconds to realize that what I saw was not an animal. My eyes still swam with color, but in the center a dark figure now moved, stepping into and out of the clear center of my vision, moving in short strides out to the river and back again toward the bank; as my sight cleared I saw that it was a woman. At the edge of the river she pulled off her skirt, looked up and down the bank, then removed her blouse and underclothes; her pale breasts fell into the sun before us. She stepped into the water. Behind our bush we were as still as dead men. She reached to her ankles, then bent forward and splashed water onto her arms.

"I could die right now," said Zoltan.

"Shhh."

"I could die right now and this would be enough."

"We shouldn't be watching this."

"She's here every day at the same time."

"She is not."

"She is too. I found her a long time ago."

"You did not."

"I did so."

I exhaled quietly, then inhaled. "You would have told me the first time you saw her. I know you, Zoltan."

He looked at me. Defeat clouded his eyes. I realized that his strength, which was assaultive and crass, depended on a weaker boy, like me: this naked woman showed me that. I turned my eyes toward shore. "Jesus, Zoltan," I whispered in a voice I lowered with awe, "she's a goddess."

He didn't answer.

"But we can't watch this."

"Who are you, Saint Edward?"

"She's going to see us."

"Shhh."

She turned and looked toward where we crouched behind the withered shrubs, then beyond us to the rising bluffs. For a single, thrilling moment, for a moment in which I felt my chest open up like a flower, I thought she had seen us; but then she dunked her head, stood again, and turned her dripping body away. "Wow," I whispered.

"Amazing grace."

"Shhh!"

"Man the lifeboats."

"Whisper, will you?"

"I'm going down with the ship."

After a time, she stepped back onto the shore, wrapped herself in a towel, and moved to the edge of the trees; we took the chance to hurry back through the shallows to the cover of the bend and sit down on the stone beach. In the distance we could still see her. She had pale skin, black hair to her waist, and a pelvis that was wide and cupped. Zoltan tried grinning at me, raising his eyebrows and curling his tongue over his lip, and I went along with it, nodding my head and smiling. But the thought of him watching her, of his joyless eyes training on her from behind the bushes, filled me, really, with sorrow. He had pockets of fat on his chest and soft arms that hung without detail from his pink shoulders, and I knew that for him the only real pleasure had been in bringing me here. We both knew it.

I myself felt something else. With Anita, on her porch and in her bedroom, a quiet world was opening to me. Now we had seen this, a view of the future. It scared Zoltan: I could see the bravado in his eyes. But it didn't scare me, Lawrence; I knew one day that the world of women would welcome me, because I knew it had welcomed you. The image of the bathing woman rose up behind my eyes, shimmering; she stood naked in the river, beckoning to me, dark and rounded, covered with the buttery shine of river water that put half moons of light into the crevices of her bones. My heart, Lawrence, felt longing like a low note of music.

"I could die right now," Zoltan said again.

That night, to celebrate, we decided to get drunk. In his room Zoltan had gathered a bottle of vodka, a bottle of gin, and a large can of frozen limeade, which he was spooning into a pitcher. It was near midnight, and I had climbed through his porch window. He broke up the frozen green lump, poured the liquor straight on top of it, covered the pitcher with his hand, and shook it.

"To love," he said.

"To love."

"I mean *real* love — to the river goddess."

"To the river goddess."

"And goodbye to the Queen."

"Well," I said. "I don't know — "

"Come on, man. We've seen the real thing."

"Okay. Goodbye to the Queen."

We drank four glasses each. Then we walked to the window, breathed deeply, and sat down. I had eaten macaroni that night, and the liquor did not creep up on me but arrived all at once. I stood and had to grip the windowsill. Soon Zoltan too had trouble standing, and we held each other up by linking one arm over the shoulder and clasping the other hand in front. We stumbled out to his hallway, past the closed room where his mother slept, down the stairs, and into the yard, where Mrs. Morris' green Impala was parked on the grass.

He held up a tangle that glinted like bass lures in the moon-light: the car keys. We got in. I found myself in the driver's seat, but after we sat this way for some time, with the key in the ignition and the windows rolled down so that the bracing puffs of river wind reached us, Zoltan got out. I pushed forward and leaned my forehead against the vinyl curve of the dash; a moment later, my door opened and he was next to me. He pushed me over on the seat and the car started. We bounced over the unpaved ruts of his driveway and drove up onto River Road.

Zoltan drove slow. I could see cracks in the asphalt. "You know, man," he said, "you have no idea what my life is like."

"Sure I do."

"No, you don't. You have no idea what it's like to be me."

The liquor rushed over me in a wave, and I waited for it to subside. I tried to breathe the river air through the open win-dow. We began to speed up. To our left stood the cliffs, and in retrospect it astonishes me that we did not go over them. The landscape dipped and spun; I looked down and saw automobile carpet, my white sneakers, Zoltan's yellow pants, and the soft gray shoe that he moved from accelerator to brake to accelera-tor. At this moment I was probably as close to him as I ever grew. He swerved to the right, but soon the car drifted left again toward the bluff, and my spine stiffened the way it did at night when I rolled near the edge of the bed. He swerved away from the cliffs, toward the fields of low grass and the shallow drain-age ditch at the side of the road. I looked at the dash: we were going forty miles an hour. I was drunk and still getting drunker. My life rested entirely in his hands, and this fact, though it should have terrified me, filled me instead with affection.

The car hit the ditch break and flew into the air. I was pitched against the corner of the dash, which came up underneath as Zoltan was thrown on top of me. The engine roared and then quieted; the car wobbled, tipped flat, and bounced when it landed. I reached up and turned off the ignition and in a moment, stumbling, we were both outside in the fields, the headlights painting an arc along the shallow tilt of the roadside ditch. Zoltan reached through the window, turned them off, and we ran.

There wasn't a lot of crime in Blue River, Lawrence, but this was exactly the kind that there was. Anyone would have done what we did next. When the police found the car, Zoltan told his mother a gang of high school dropouts had stolen it; he even had a pretty good idea of who had done the driving. After church the next morning, he pulled up his corduroys and showed me a purple ridge along the length of his shin: he was going to spend the rest of the summer in long pants. A tender spot in my shoulder had stiffened; I had awakened that morning unable to lift my arm.

I waited two days, called Mrs. Morris to say I had heard about the car accident, and told her that you and I fixed cars all the time. We would do a professional job; all she had to do was buy a few cans of body filler and have the car towed to our yard. On the phone her voice swelled with feeling. It wasn't saving the money, she said; it was having friends like us.

She pulled into our driveway the following Saturday morning, the bumper dragging, and we started working on it that afternoon. You quickly made a plan of the work: we would drill a set of holes along the five or six shallow creases and the single deep one, straighten them with the puller, fill in with body plastic, and then paint. We took turns drilling; even this was tiring, lining up a hundred holes in the Impala's green panels, but by evening we had pulled it into rough shape and coarsened the paint with files so that the filler would take.

You had said little through the day. Finally, after putting away the drill, you turned to me and spoke. "Were you drunk?"

"Who?"

"You," you said. "When you crashed this baby."

"Thieves crashed it."

You chuckled. "What do you take me for, Ed?"

I pulled a lump of body paste from the can. "What makes you think it was us?"

You smirked. At the time, Lawrence, this confirmed what I had long suspected: that I had no secrets from you. You seemed to possess a shared knowledge of everything I did or could imagine doing. I spooned the lump into the dent and shaped it with two fast strokes of the spreader. "What about Mom?" I said. "Does she know?"

"Depends what you mean."

"Come on, Lawrence."

You leaned forward and looked at my work. "Build it up more," you said. "Sand it later."

"Come on."

"She could know if she wanted to."

"You didn't say anything to Dary?"

You looked at me and sat down on the grass. "Listen," you said, "I told you before. You better watch yourself with that Zoltan kid. First he's dropping matches; now he's parking the car in ditches. He's going to kill you both."

"We were going ten miles an hour."

You put your finger in the crease of the quarter panel. "They don't make steel like they used to, I guess."

"We were going a little faster."

"A *little*?"

"It was dark. We drove into a ditch that's two feet deep."

"They had to winch the car out, Ed."

"Okay, we might have been going *a lot* faster."

You picked up the body mallet and swung the long hickory shaft a couple of times into your bad hand. "Let me tell you something, Ed," you said. "There are two kinds of people in the world, and Zoltan's the kind who wants to kill himself."

"It was an accident."

"But *he* was driving."

"How do you know?"

"I just do. You wouldn't drive the car into a ditch. You're not that kind of person."

"There are lots of kinds of people, Lawrence."

"No, there're not, Ed." You smiled. "There are two."

"Am I spreading this thick enough?"

You leaned forward. "Fine." You ran your hand through your hair, then tapped me on the knee. "You're the other kind, by the way."

The paste had begun to harden on the spreader blade. I scraped at it with my fingernail. To this day, Lawrence, I still wonder if what you told me then is true. "What kind of person am I?" I said.

"The kind who wants to kill someone else."

"*I* am?"

"Yeah."

"I don't want to kill anybody."

"Yes, you do."

"Hah!"

"That's why you hang out with Zoltan."

"*What?*"

"Recognize the truth when it's before you."

I looked up. "I hang out with Zoltan because we're friends."

"Who are *you* kidding? You want to kill him and he wants to kill himself; that's it. That's why you're together. You don't even like him."

"You're crazy," I said. "That's crazy." And it still does seem crazy to me, Lawrence, most of the time. I stirred the paste. "I don't like him that much," I said, "but I don't want to *kill* him. *That's* the truth." I picked up the spreader and pushed it into the dent. "Maybe some people want to kill people, but not me. I just want to fix the car."

"That's your mistake."

"How can that be a mistake?"

"Look," you said, "I'm telling you that *all* people are either one or the other. Either they want to kill themselves or they want to kill another person. I'm saying it's true about every single person."

"You're crazy, Lawrence."

"Maybe."

I stood and moved away to get a look at the panel. Beyond us a group of robins picked at the lawn. It seemed to me in those days that a person could know a lot about cars or American history or electricity, but that nobody knew any more than anybody else about human beings. I came back to the Impala and dug the spoon into the can of filler. Your back was turned toward the car, your small waist and asymmetrical shoulders, and suddenly it became clear that I wanted you to leave us.

You shook your head in a gesture of impatience. "That's a better education than you're going to get in school," you said. "So you ought to thank me."

In late July, Mr. Howland gave the annual Community Club dinner in his living room. I had never been in his house before, and that day I discovered it was a century-old mansion a mile out of town, built to resemble a riverboat and backed against the bluff where its three-sided widow's walk looked out over the river. Several imposing columns faced the street. Thick

wooden caps carved into lions' heads supported the overhanging second story, where rows of round windows cut the siding
like portholes. Mr. Howland had picked us up in the Community Club van and taken us out in two trips. I was in the first
group, which arrived at his house while the sun, still well above
the horizon but already tinged with its setting red, reflected a
willow and a giant elm in the huge windows by the door. We
filed in shyly and stood in the hall. Small spectrums of sunlight
from the high windows painted jewels on the plaster walls. Mr.
Howland left to pick up the other members of the club while
the rest of us moved to his dark living room and found chairs.
They were carved, with petal patterns and smaller versions of
the lions' heads we had seen outside. Twelve of us sat there, six
boys in ties and six girls in dresses, and nobody spoke. I whis-
tled the opening of the Bellini concerto. Zoltan buried his
hands in his pockets.

Presently, from the back of the house, came the hum of Lottie's wheelchair. We sat silently while the click and high whine
and the rubbery skid of direction changes grew louder down a
corridor, and I felt in my gut the bloom of panic. As the wheelchair turned into the well-lighted front hall and her boxlike
shadow appeared at the doorway, I felt the urge to bolt: out
through the front door, down the wooden ramp, across the
elmed and willowed yard until I was in the fields across the
road where I belonged, standing in the hot, brown dirt. She
coughed and drove out onto the carpet among us. Her pink silk
blouse was tied in front with a heavy hanging bow, and a red
scarf lay on her shoulders; she had set her hair. Marian Kremer,
a popular, flirtatious girl in the group, laughed, and Lottie
stopped short. She looked up, flushed. The pale cord of her hearing aid caught in her collar so that she had to swing her head to
free it, looking, as she did so, from face to face. Her legs were
hidden by their blanket.

"Oh, Lottie," said Anita. "We're all so happy you're here."
Zoltan snickered.

"We are," I said.

"We're fortunate to have you here in the house," said Lottie, looking from side to side again across the room.

"We should have this here every year," said Anita. She made a show of admiring the room. "Your house is so beautiful."

"Thank you." She pressed the controls and the chair bumped and pivoted, the wheels turning from one direction to another. Then she glided forward to the low armoire against the far wall. It was dark wood, like the chairs, and carved in scrolls along its edges. I looked at a painting of two deer by a waterfall. Lottie turned her neck to face us, her chin dropping slightly with the motion so that she had to look up to meet our eyes. "My father won't be back for a few minutes," she said, "so why don't we enjoy ourselves?"

Her voice was composed, in every way a normal voice except for the exaggerated motion of her larynx, which bumped out and retracted, chickenlike, as she spoke. Everything else about her was queer and tragic — her limbs, her ears, the parted stance of her lips. She opened the armoire door.

"We *are* enjoying ourselves," said Anita.

Lottie pivoted in the chair, and when she turned away from the armoire she held a crystal decanter in her hand, almost full, topped with a crystal plug. Lawrence, I see now that more than anything else she wanted to be like us, to take part in our ordinary, base pleasures, and I suppose this makes it easier to accept what happened. She opened the decanter, tilted it to her lips, and drank for several seconds, her throat bobbing the way it did when she spoke. Then she came toward me. I suppose she chose me because I was familiar to her. Her chair slid across the carpet, her face pressed forward, intent on mine, the decanter held up in front of her. She reached me and put it in my hands.

What was I going to do? The others were silent while Lottie, born unlucky, sat before me, marked with the jittery eyes and mouth of an animal. I tilted back the bottle and drank. The bourbon dried my tongue, and when I swallowed, first one large gulp and then another, it burned a track that I could feel inside my body, throat to belly. I turned and handed the decanter to Zoltan.

He drank quickly and passed it on. It traveled twice around the circle, each of us taking fast gulps, even Anita, whose eyelids closed and fluttered as she swallowed. Across from me in a white blouse and a blue skirt whose pleats had been ironed to crispness, she drank, brushed her mouth with the back of her hand, then drank again. She was flushed. Lottie had the bottle now, and she moved toward the armoire. As she opened the door, its lion's face swinging toward me to reveal a whole row of identical crystal decanters, the sound of the van reached us from out front. She replaced the bottle and closed the cabinet. She passed around a roll of peppermint Life Savers, and then the other Community Club members were making their way across the darkened lawn and into the house. Soon Mr. Howland's thick shoulders filled the living room doorway, where he stood watching as the new arrivals found seats. He surveyed us, his black hair falling partway over his forehead.

"God's children," he whispered.

It was at this moment, with the liquor still stinging in my throat, that I had my first understanding of him, Lawrence. He was a suspecter, I realized right then, a detective of guilt: evil led him forward. I coughed. Across from me, Anita's pale cheeks were blotched with red and her eyes were cast to the floor. Marian Kremer stared at the wall. Only Zoltan showed no sign of guilt. He looked around the room, his face raised, his pudgy mouth curved up. I felt a bolt of respect and gratefulness for the hard core of his character. Mr. Howland's method was to accuse and then wait for a sign; Zoltan, now, gave none. He leaned forward and his fat belly jiggled. I smiled; Mr. Howland met my gaze and for a moment his dark eyes narrowed. Then he moved slowly across the living room. "Let's eat," he said, touching our shoulders, ruffling our hair with his huge palms.

We ate that night in his living room and his yard-sized kitchen, twenty of us seated on his carved chairs, eating Sloppy Joes from big tins spread across the tables. He had set out bowls of salad and cartons of cream soda, and after dinner he came around with a cardboard box of fudge ice pops, smiling at each of us as we pulled them from the box, looking at us as though the speed or courtesy of our grasps was the clue he had been searching for in our personalities. I thanked him and pulled a pop gently from the front. He smiled at me, leaned down, and at the moment he came closest to me, his breath hoarse and his thick eyebrows arched, he pursed his mouth and sniffed.

Then he moved on. When we had finished dessert he showed us around the downstairs of the house, where, on the hallway wall, framed neatly and mounted in a line that went from living room to kitchen, kitchen to staircase, staircase to landing, hung a dozen antique etchings. They were brown ink on faded, clothlike paper, and as he led us through the hall he paused in front of each and insisted we examine the fine detail, so excruciatingly small that to me the artist seemed mad. A man in a top hat holding a carved cane stood on the steps of a theater, happy-looking and fat — and only by leaning forward, my nostrils fogging little circles on the dusted glass, could I see his hair falling below the hat brim: hundreds of miniature snakes stranding from his scalp, each tongue forked and extended. They had been etched with a magnifying glass, Mr. Howland told us; he brought out several jeweler's lenses and we stood in the hallway, bending toward the pictures. A woman's eyelashes, each one intricately drawn, were miniature flames; the simian crease on a man's palm, its narrow cleavage shaded with a written word inscribed twenty times across the hand, said CREED; a wound, open on a soldier's leg, crawled with maggots that through the jeweler's lens were composed of a hundred narrow-necked bottles — of bourbon, we presumed.

After Mr. Howland finished showing us the house, the girls began to stack the dirty dishes at the sink, sending them one by one along a bridge of hands, where they were scraped and washed and dried. I helped put them in the glass-fronted cabinets, each plate clinking delicately. I laid them edge first, touching the flower-painted rims together, rolling each one softly onto the ceramic belly of the one below it. When the plates were done and the girls at the sink started on the glasses and the silverware, I went out by myself to the back porch. This far out of town there were no streetlights, only the candle-like glow of the intermittent bluff houses across in Minnesota, and above me the black sky that lay chocked with stars. I sat down on the sloping door of the storm cellar. The liquor no longer lightened my head, but my muscles felt soft and my mind was loose with a confessional ease. I felt apart. Behind me, through the walls of the house, the Community Club clinked and stacked and arranged the glasses and cutlery. I thought of our mother and Mrs. Silver in our own kitchen; they, too, would chat while they cleaned, and a listener sitting outside the house would hear the highlights of their conversation, the nouns — Husband, Retirement, Damnation — for which the talk paused and floated outside. Here, crouching on the storm cellar of Mr. Howland's house, I listened to the sounds of dishes and of blurred, fleeting talk, now miraculously coming from girls my own age. Below me the river currents turned over themselves, burying and uncovering starlight.

When Mr. Howland came out, he stopped on the stairs behind me without speaking. I knew who it was from the inhale followed by the pause, which was peculiar to him, before the exhale. He walked down and stood next to me. A shooting star flamed and disappeared in front of us, so low along the horizon that it seemed to pass over the far side of the earth. He stepped around to where I could see him. His face was unmoving, the level eyes looking into mine — his old man's trick — and I realized that he was trying to take advantage of the meteor. He stared, unblinking.

"Thank you for the dinner," I said.

"The dinner," he repeated, letting out his breath. He inhaled again and paused. "Sellers," he said. "You really bust me."

"Sir?"

"What went on in there tonight?"

"What do you mean?"

"I mean, who do you think I am? Do you think I don't know what went on?"

I turned and looked across his yard. There were no lights behind us, and in the distance among the wild birch the black grew deeper. Beyond that, at the horizon, it grew deeper yet, but there it was blue-tinged, the color of the deep, deep night. Why was he talking to *me*? Why was I the one he accused, out here among the falling scraps of galaxy? My throat burned. "I'd like to help you," I said.

He folded his hands as I looked at him. "You would, would you?"

"Yes, sir."

"Then tell me what went on in there."

"Nothing much, really. Not much, sir."

"Not much?"

He put his finger into his mouth, where he picked absently at a tooth, and suddenly, right then, as he held his other hand steady in the air between us, I knew he was talking to me because I was the one who would betray my friends. I knew this,

Lawrence, and the knowledge came upon me like a wave. He knew it too, and he knew I had nowhere near the strength to resist him. I turned away and looked over the river.

"We drank your bourbon," I said finally.

"You did," he said, "didn't you?"

"Yes, sir."

A pause grew. "Did my daughter —" he said, "did Lottie have anything to do with this?"

Along the palisade the tree leaves showed silver, rustled, then showed black. I turned toward him, but his gaze was averted and in the air between us his hand had begun to shake. I looked away. "No," I said at last. "She had nothing to do with it."

I saw him turn again toward me. I shifted on the cellar door and gazed up into the jeweled Wisconsin sky, and at that moment, as my head was lifted toward the heavens to hide my lie, he reached across and laid his palm on my forehead. "She is all the world to me," he said softly; and we stayed like that for a few moments, as though this were a benediction, as though there were love or communication between us, until someone called him from inside and the gentle weight of his hand lifted.

That week, Lyna Melner's old house burned. Just after dark, the sirens came from town, the low honk and scream of the hook-and-ladder rumbling a quarter mile away, the mixture of its pitches seeming to shake the whole earth. River wind was blowing. Downstream along the palisade I heard the trucks gathering, and up in the star-pocked sky I saw a cloudy haze of light. The treetops, the low-pitched aluminum roofs, the air itself took on the hint of color.

I ran across the yard, out past the shanty, through the gap in the hedge to the sloping path at the edge of the land; my feet pounded, my ankles caught on sticks and ruts. Others ran with me; their voices welled and disappeared in the darkness. The path filled, and I was darting in and out, touching the roughcut fence for bearing while from everywhere around me — from the woods to the east and the river to the west and the sloping path in front — from everywhere came the crackling of two-way radios and the thrum of distant engines. A siren stopped; soon we were close. I came through a clearing and glimpsed faces: people carrying blankets and thermoses, a man with a bucket. The other sirens stopped, and suddenly I could hear the rush of the fire itself, like breathing. The wood popped and hissed. I drew close and saw the flames, not huge yet but seething, forming and unforming, darts of yellow-orange poking from windows across the second floor. A gust came up, moved through the trees, and when it reached the house the flames paused, then rushed out again, reaching through the window frames up toward the roof. A ladder, angled from the truck, moved up there. The hoses sprayed from above. I stood at the high border of the hill behind the Melners' yard and watched the cascading water. Steam billowed where it hit, rose in the sky in huge clouds that turned orange, then black, then white as they climbed high up out of the light and into the dark dome of the night.

"The Melners'," someone said.

"Elaine and Jim."

"Where are the children?"

"All gone."

"Lyna's in Chicago."

"That house is all wood."

"It was empty; they're in Florida."

The water hissed down. It streamed from the windows and the cracks in the wall. From underneath the billowing clouds, flames reached up again. Two firemen stood in the front porch with axes. They swung, and the door was down. For a moment we could see the Melners' coat rack, a painting of geese on the wall, the light green rug in the entrance hall — and then smoke poured through the doorframe. The men went in. People gasped. Through the smoke we saw their legs, the yellow stripes of their coats, their axes pumping while a hose moved down toward them. Water sprayed, smoke billowed and then in a few seconds cleared so that we saw the entrance hall again, smokeless for an instant, the rug and painting still there, the coat rack now alight with flame. In a moment water smothered it.

I moved down closer to where hoses as thick as logs crossed the lawn from the pump truck. The firemen were making progress, the flames gradually falling beneath the torrent of water. In a half hour they had turned to slate-colored smoke that rolled from the windows and gathered above us in a cloud as big as the house. Now and then they erupted again, sheets of orange fanning out from the windows, as though the fire itself were alive and desperate, moving to the back of the house when the main hose moved to the front, forming again in the basement when the firemen sprayed the roof. I found myself rooting for it, but soon it came only as an orange reflection in the smoke, no longer reaching through the windows but still rising every few moments inside the gaping walls. I stood in the heat, sweating. By ten o'clock all but one of the engines were gone, and then the smoke changed color, no longer gray but white, like steam, rising steadily from every window and broken wall in the house, and in another hour the fire was out.

The next day I went over with Zoltan to see the charred framing and queer views of rugs and armchairs and a bed, still made, that poked through the hacked-down walls above us. I watched him scrupulously, my heart burning with dread and excitement. He didn't seem surprised; he didn't seem nervous. He nodded his head and narrowed his eyes as we examined the house from the hill flank. We walked down and stood in the yard, and when Zoltan stepped up onto the crumbling porch steps, he slipped and fell. Everything was slick with wet ashes. "Some hot one," he finally said, standing up.

"It was huge, man."

"Pretty big from the looks of it."

"I knew the girl who lived there."

He rubbed the ashes from his sleeve. "No one lived there," he said.

I looked at him. "She used to. She was a friend of my sister's. Lyna Melner. She got knocked up." I tossed a stone. "How come you didn't come down?"

He shrugged and moved away into the yard. "I didn't feel like it."

"It was huge, man."

"I've seen bigger."

"So have I, but it was something."

"They all look big. Old wood burns hot."

I ran my hands through my hair. "My brother looked around," I said. "He thinks it started in more than one place."

"So?"

"So," I said. I picked up a stone and tossed it. "That's what arsonists do."

"Your brother work for the fire department now too?"

"He knows a lot about that kind of stuff, Morris."

"He thinks he knows a lot about everything."

"He knows a lot, Zoltan."

"Bullshit, Sellers."

I picked up another stone. I threw it at the burned frame, then threw another one, harder, at a broken window on the second floor. I missed. Zoltan lurched one underhanded, and it didn't hit anything. The next stone I threw shattered a corner of glass, and the next one too. "Well, I don't know, Morris," I said. "I mean, this was someone's *house*."

Sometimes it seemed to me that you had planned your own life, Lawrence, that you had sown it in rows like a field, so that later, in exactitude, it would appear before you. I wonder how much of what we knew of you in those years — the years you moved so calmly through the world — was an invention. "Always do what you're afraid of," you once told me. Do you remember saying that? More or less, I now believe, it was the creed of your existence. Before the days of your wildness, as our mother used to call that time, you had been the shyest of boys — rather tall, thinner than you should have been, disposed toward hiding in the ventilation space below the house and in the twisted boughs of trees. To become what you did then — a boy with a stolen wardrobe in your closet and raised scars on your knuckles — must have taken the same discipline you later drew on to rectify your life. Your courage was solitary, that of a timid boy who had learned to force his way. You were made of willful change, and now, suddenly, you changed again.

Why did it happen then? I have thought many times about your life, Lawrence, about its arc, which rose and broke like a wave, about why the timetable of your demise was as it was: yet I cannot clearly see the answer. In that time, I myself was in my earliest preparation for leaving our family. Was that it? Or was it, as I thought after my medical training, genetic — the clock in every cell of your body? The morning after the fire, you opened the window to your basement apartment and called me in from where I'd been sitting at the base of our oak, absently screening the ground for Yellow Nightshine. I crossed the yard, and when I entered the room found you lying on your stomach in bed, your face buried in the pillow; next to you, a shape pushed up the bedclothes.

She was mostly covered by the blanket, her back toward me, but I could see the flesh-colored cord of her hearing aid curling over the top of her head. What was happening to you, Lawrence? What could you have meant by calling me in? You turned your head to look at me. My eyes followed the line where her misshapen body pushed up the bedding. I saw the protruding hip, twisted at its queer angle, the small tapering ridge of blanket where her diminished legs ran, the thick, shining canopy of hair that even then, I noticed, was beautiful. It spilled over the folded edge of the sheet. At that moment she turned and I saw for an instant her pale, parted lips before I moved my eyes to you. Your arm lay on her shoulder. You shifted again and faced into the sheets. "Ed," you said, "Lottie needs help."

"Jesus Christ, Lawrence."

"She needs help getting to her chair."

"Jesus, Jesus Christ."

"Lawrence," came her voice from the pillow, "please don't do this."

"Be a gentleman, Ed," you said softly.

"I'm getting out of here, Lawrence."

Your voice hardened. "Put the chair outside first. I want you to be a gentleman."

I saw it then in the corner, pushed against the wall. I understand now that your life was ruled by forces I will never imagine. What should I have done? Of course I should have left, but I had neither the foresight nor the strength of character to disobey you. Instead, I moved to the corner, lifted the wheelchair, and set it at the top of the short stairs at the door. Then I crossed over and stood on Lottie's side of the sagging mattress.

She tangled with the bedclothes, and I saw that her dress had been pulled up around her neck. It was blue cotton, bunched at her shoulders, and when she reached her hand up to smooth it, my heart dropped in my chest. Wriggling, she pulled the dress down. She looked past me, and her eyes were wet. Maybe I should have walked away, Lawrence: I could have gone up the stairs into the bright yard and begun, right then, my efforts to be free of you; but instead, in a stiff and embarrassed gesture, I bent over and extended my arms, and she, shrugging, turned and rolled into them.

To this day, I can recall the lightness of her body as it came up in my grasp. So little was left of her that I lifted her almost to my shoulders. From the waist up, she was a normal girl — a woman — but starting with her flattened and emaciated pelvis and extending down the unformed, stringy legs — her braces lay next to the chair — she was no larger than a child. The smell of her powder rose. Her body, settling into my arms, flattened across my chest like a bag of flour. Her hair fell about my shoulders. I was grateful for the way it spread itself to hide her there, like a veil, so that we would not have to see each other. I crossed the room and climbed the stairs, and at the top I set her in the chair.

"How's that?" I said.

"Fine."

"Are you okay, Lottie?"

"Fine."

"You're heavier than I thought," I said. "I mean that as a compliment; I just didn't expect it."

"Thank you."

"I mean, you're still *light*."

"Edward, I know exactly what I am."

Her back was to me and she was lifting her legs and placing them in the stirrups. We still hadn't looked at each other. I blinked in the bright light and knew that from then on our relations would be governed by what she had just said. I knew that we would never speak of this: that was the way we were. In the yard she smoothed her dress again and wheeled quickly along the side alley, around the corner of the house, and out to the sidewalk, the chair audible all the way up the block as I watched it disappear, and even after that, like an airplane in the distance, as I stood there, listening to it move away toward town.

I could not go back to your room right away, so I returned to the yard. Why would you seduce a crippled girl, pulling her dress up over her shoulders? My gorge rose. I leaned against the oak and on its rough bark could feel the beating of my heart. I imagined Mr. Howland in his yard, his thick finger shaking. I had never in my life considered you despicable, Lawrence, but for a few moments while I hugged the tree, that is what I thought.

When I finally returned to your room, you were still in bed, staring at the ceiling. The smell of liquor was clearer now. "Jesus Christ, Lawrence, you've really done it."

"You mad about something, Ed?"

"I don't know. Maybe not."

"Not sure, huh?"

"Maybe I am."

"About what?"

"How could you do that?"

You pushed down the sheets and I looked out the window at the tracks of her chair on the dewy grass.

"Maybe it's the kind of person I am," you said.

"Come on, Lawrence."

"She liked it enough, anyway." You sat up in bed. "Besides, Ed, it was an act of mercy."

"Hah!"

"It might be the nicest thing I've ever done."

"That doesn't say much for you."

"It doesn't?"

"No."

"I don't know, Ed. I think it does. What have you ever done that's as merciful?"

"What have *I* ever done?"

You didn't say anything. I sat on the bed and inhaled the scents. "I've done lots of things. All the stuff at the Community Club, for one."

You laughed, and after a few moments, I laughed too. You reached up and put your hand on my shoulder.

"God, it must have been pretty weird," I said.

"Sort of."

"I don't know, Lawrence."

"What don't you know?"

"Whether it was such a hot idea."

"You're a philosopher now?" You put your head back on the pillow.

"Can she, umm, feel anything?"

"Maybe not," you said, yawning. "Maybe she was just singing." You smiled.

"Singing?" I looked at you. "Oh."

We both smiled. Then you closed your eyes and, while I stood there, you feigned sleep. You were breathing coarsely through your nose, a fake snore. It seemed to me that if you returned to your old ways, you would be headed for serious trouble this time. Lottie's red scarf lay on the windowsill, and I went over and picked it up. "You'll end up like Lyna Melner," I whispered, and though your head was turned away, I saw you smile once more.

But whatever had bubbled over in you that day seemed to disappear immediately. We didn't talk anymore about what happened, and when you lectured to us at the Community Club the next week, you leaned into the microphone and spoke like a man of God. You waved your fingers over us and whispered. Lottie was there, and Mr. Howland stood in the corner with her, rubbing his gruff chin as you spoke, his other arm on the handle of her chair. When you finished, you walked over and shook his hand.

3

WHEN I CONSIDER YOUR ACTIONS NOW, Lawrence, I think I understand what your intentions were. You, as always, could not forget a slight, and Henry Howland — in your eyes, at least — had more than slighted us. He had humbled you — the years you worked for him, I now see, were humiliation — but what mattered even more to you, I also see, was that he had once hurt our mother.

Did you expect Lottie to tell her father what had happened? I still don't know, and I don't know either whether Lottie did tell him. But one morning after the Community Club, Mr. Howland stopped me in the basement hallway of St. Vitus. "Mr. Sellers," he said, as I sauntered out of our meeting, "don't we have something to talk about?"

"Yes, sir," I said. "I guess so."

"Well, then. Let's."

Heat was wilting the roses outside the ground-level windows; he brushed a pane with his forearm and leaned against it. "Go ahead," he said. "Tell me."

"Tell you what?"

He came forward from the window and examined me, his eyes blinking. He didn't say anything else, Lawrence; he just stared, and after a few moments I realized it wasn't a trick this time; it was something else. The big lashes curtained the orbs, which were shiny now. At that moment, through the heavy oak beams and the plaster ceiling, through the mortised floorboards and the thick carpet of the offices, I heard the starting lurch of Lottie's wheelchair and its creaking slide across the up stairs hallway. Mr. Howland blinked again and looked away. Tiny drops beaded his lashes. It seemed right to me that this was how he would cry — with half-tears, blinking. I turned away. I would not reconsider him until years later, until after your influence on me had waned, and at the time I still disliked him. But there he was: weeping. I knew why. I touched his arm.

"Edward Sellers," he said, looking out the window into the rose stems, "did your brother bring shame to my family?"

"Did he what?"

"You understand."

I coughed. "I don't know everything my brother does," I said.

"I need you to tell me."

I looked out the low window above us. If Lottie had told him, why was he asking me? Was I to lie to him again? Through the clots of earth and the low shrubs across the yard I saw the tapered rise of St. Vitus's spire, and I knew that I was moving farther and farther from faith. I coughed again to gain time. This *shame* he spoke of — it was, after all, what he himself had brought to *our* family. But I didn't say this, and as I shuffled in front of him, repeating the word in my head, I thought only of its oddness: it was a disguised word, the word of a clergyman. I glanced back at him. He was not moving, almost not breathing, looking away from me. I had just begun to see the world as retributive and pulling and unexemplary.

"No, sir," I said. "He didn't."

I was watching his face reflected in the glass door at the end of the hall: relief burst over him. I don't think I had ever heard him laugh before, but as he stepped away from the window, that was what he did — he laughed — and then he bent toward me to ruffle my hair with his palm.

That night Zoltan told me he wanted to introduce himself to the woman we had seen on the shore. "It's our only chance," he said.

"Chance?"

He grinned. "I've been back a bunch of times," he said. He winked. "God helps those who help themselves."

"Zoltan, that's a religious expression."

"Don't be a skeezer."

"It's about righteousness."

"Forgive me, Father."

"I just don't think we can do it."

"We have to, Sellers. Don't you see? It's a gift from God. We have to introduce ourselves." He smiled. There was fear in his eyes. "She's a creature of heaven."

"Who are we now," I said, "Samuel Taylor Coleridge?"

"Who?"

"She'll shriek, Morris."

"Maybe."

"She will for sure."

"Not the way *I* do it."

"How's that, Casanova?"

"You'll see."

"What are you going to do?"

"I'll walk out there and introduce myself."

"Hah!"

"I will. But I'll do something else, too."

"What?"

"You'll see."

"She'll run, you idiot."

"No, she won't. I'll just introduce myself."

"You don't know girls, Zoltan."

He narrowed his eyes. "I suppose *you* do?"

"Better than you, at least."

"I know what I'm doing, man." He put his hands in his pockets. "Just watch me."

The next morning we went out to wait for her: we were going to unroll our lives like rugs. But that day she didn't come, nor the next one; and by the third day I was ready to quit. When I saw the desperate cheer in Zoltan's eyes, though, I stayed. I lay down in the water that morning and tried to go to sleep. Next to me, he remained standing, half concealed by the dying shrubs. Near noon, I heard a gasp, and when I looked up, his shoulders had stiffened as though he'd been shot: she was emerging from the trees. He brushed the waveless surface back and forth with his foot, and when she crossed the hilltop and began her stroll down to the water, he drew in his breath, held it, and seemed to make a physical effort to calm himself. He stood motionless while she came down to the sand, stripped, and walked into the river, and then, with a swiftness I had never seen in him before, he pulled off his own shirt and pants and underwear, gave a soft, high-pitched grunt, and stepped around the bend.

"You're going to kill yourself, Zoltan," I whispered.

His body cupped and pocked and jiggled, rolled over itself as he stepped slowly before me through the shallows. I had never seen him naked. His skin was the color of sand and gleamed with sweat. He lifted each foot clear of the water, pulled each arm all the way through with his stride. "Come back," I whispered. He turned and squinted at me, then righted himself and continued on his way. He made no splash or noise. Twenty yards ahead of him she stretched skyward, arched her back, leaned forward, and splashed water over her body. He stepped, planted, lifted his foot; he stepped again. Ten yards from him now her arms dripped diamonds. I breathed in, swallowed, pressed my hands together. She looked up. He stopped. Before him, her arms held sideways, she let her face rise to level and then ceased all motion. They stared at each other like deer. I breathed in, breathed out. A swallow darted down over the water, skimmed crazily, and shot up again. Downriver a motorboat chugged. Then she looked down again, leaned forward, and, as if she had never seen him, went on splashing herself.

In an instant he was crashing back through the shallows, and then we were running downriver on the shore, Zoltan windmilling his pale arms as he stumbled and righted himself on the rocks, the clothes he had snatched up flapping in his hands like flags. We ran past all the bends and coves, past the rising path to his house and the marshy patch of inlets at the edge of town, and we slowed only at the deep water upriver of the dock, stopping finally at the last curve before the marina. We sat on a log and he dressed himself. With each breath he coughed, and each time I slapped him on the back.

"Sellers," he whispered between coughs.

"What got into your head?"

"Hoo-wee!" he shouted.

"What a charmer."

"Yowee, yowee!"

He had a fit of coughing that lasted several minutes, and then he quieted down. Dread was building in me. He put on his socks and shoes and we stood staring out over the river. The boat I had heard moved past us upstream.

"Sellers."

"Morris."

"Jesus H."

We stood there until the boat was gone from sight. A few feet out a big carp turned curves below the surface, and I watched it until Zoltan's breathing was calm again. Now and then he coughed. We said nothing further, and it wasn't until much later that I realized what a great defeat this had been for him.

"You know," I said to you a couple of days later as we were priming the filled dents of the Impala. "Mr. Howland asked me what happened with Lottie."

"Yeah?" You were feathering the edges.

"He asked me after Community Club."

"You know," you said, "maybe we should get Dary to paint this."

"Why Dary?"

"She'd do a better job. You have to match the shade exactly. It's faded."

We looked at the border where pale green met the unpainted filler. I waited for you to speak. You shook the can of primer until the ball rattled, then passed it in quick strokes across the panel.

"Do you want to know whether I told him?" I said.

"I know you didn't."

"How do you know that?"

"How do I know?" You made another pass with the spray

can. "Because I know *you*. You want to think you wouldn't tell." You looked up at the house and waved your arm. In a few moments Darienne came out.

"I almost did tell him," I said.

"You will eventually. You *will* tell him."

"Yes?" said Darienne.

"I will not."

"We need you to match the paint job."

"You want *me* to paint your car?"

"You'd do the best job, Dary. We need your eye."

She looked down at the panel, then hiked up her skirt, squatted, and ran her finger along the edge of the prime coat. I saw the pleasure moving everywhere through her, like blood; I saw that she would always forgive us. "Well," she said, "it won't be easy. Let's see the color you have."

You shook the can of green paint and sprayed a small stroke over the primer. We all looked at it.

"You don't know everything I'm going to do and not do, Lawrence," I said.

You laughed. "Yes, I do, Ed."

"What are you two fighting about now?" said Darienne. She dipped her finger in the thinner you held and touched it to the green stroke on the panel. We watched it lighten as she hummed the opening of the Bellini. "Boy," she said, "you guys sure are lucky there's a girl around."

"You *will* tell him," you said. You offered her the jar of thinner. "Trust me."

"Tell him what?" said Darienne.

"Maybe if I had really wanted to kill someone, I would have told him."

"I give up," said Darienne.

That morning we sanded the quarter panels until we couldn't discern where the metal met the filler. Then Darienne used paint thinner and rags to smooth the old and new colors together until the borders were invisible. We looked from every angle and still couldn't detect the seams. The next evening, Mrs. Morris came over to pick up the car, scrutinizing it while I pointed out the flawless work. You stood behind us, cleaning your tools. Darienne hovered next to Mrs. Morris, brushing away dust on the paint with her finger.

"You men do beautiful work," said Mrs. Morris.

"What do you think of the paint job?" said Darienne.

Mrs. Morris leaned down to examine it. "I can't tell where they painted. It looks perfect to me."

"It's a good job," I said.

Darienne glared at me. Finally, I said, "Darienne did the painting, Mrs. Morris."

"She did?" She tilted her head. "Well, it's pretty good." She touched it with her finger and narrowed her eyes. "It's just a *little* bit off there; otherwise it's excellent."

Darienne approached. "No, it's not," she said. "It's perfect."

"Well," she said, "it's *good*, but it's not quite perfect."

"Where's it off?"

Mrs. Morris brushed her hand over an area of the panel and Darienne bent to examine it. I did too, over their shoulders, and I saw that indeed it was perfect. I wondered what it was about my sister that brought on criticism.

"Did they ever catch who crashed it?" you called from the tool shanty.

"Did they what?" said Mrs. Morris.

"Catch the jokers who crashed the car?"

"You know," I said, leaning down, "you might be right. It's just a little bit lighter where Darienne painted it. You can barely see it."

"What?" said Darienne. She widened her eyes at me. "You just said it was perfect."

"I never said that, Dary. *You* did. It's just a little bit off."

"Just a bit," said Mrs. Morris.

The next afternoon, I went out on the attic roof to see Darienne, where she was painting our oak tree. She sat perched on the eaves with her easel resting across her knees. The foreground of the canvas was already filled in with an enlarged gnarled bough and the shingles sloping away to the gutter.

"I wanted to tell you I'm sorry," I said.

"It's too late."

"Your paint job *was* perfect."

"Then how come you said it wasn't?"

"I don't know," I said. "I was just being polite."

She brushed yellow into the bark of the bough, which made it suddenly appear solid. "Well, you weren't being polite."

"Jeez," I said, leaning down close to the canvas. "That's good."

"You just didn't want to talk about who did it."

I stood up. "What are you talking about?"

"You know what I mean."

"No, I don't."

"I mean, who wrecked her car."

"It was stolen."

She dabbed at the palette. "If I had to paint the bruise you have on your shoulder, Edward, I'd use a lot of violet and yellow." She touched the brush to the canvas. "The yellow would make it disturbing."

"What are you saying?"

"Edward," she said, "why do you lie to me? Why do you treat me like I'm not part of your life? You and Lawrence, you and Lawrence, you think you have this secret little smart thing between you. I know you wrecked the car."

I walked to the edge of the shingles. The gutters at my feet were clogged with years of leaves. I wondered if Mrs. Morris knew, too: I wondered if Zoltan and I had fooled *anybody*. How could everyone so easily see through my own life, when I, looking at yours, saw only what you showed me?

"How come you didn't let on?" I said to Darienne.

"That's not how I am. Not everyone's like Lawrence, you know. That's not how you run a family. I know a lot more than you think. One day you'll see." She touched the brush to the palette. "That paint job was perfect," she said. "It was perfect."

"I admit it."

"You know, you ought to be more honest with me. You know that? You can talk to me if you're in trouble. I'm your sister, remember? If you wreck a car, you can tell me." She began painting the leaves.

"I suppose so."

"I mean, we're going to have to, pretty soon. It's going to be you and me."

"What's going to be you and me?"

She didn't answer, and I sat down with my feet over the edge. In the distant limbs of the oak two robins were darting. I watched their dizzying ascents and their softened plummets, downward, from branch to branch. They chattered. They beat their wings and hopped, jerked their beaks and scratched at the bark. I looked higher in the tree and found what they were trying to distract me from: a small nest, hidden in the upper twigs. "Sometimes I think — you know," I said. "Sometimes I think Lawrence is funny."

"He *is*," she said.

"You think so?"

"I know so. I've seen it." She set down her brush and looked at me. "I mean Lawrence is more than funny, Edward. He might be a little crazy."

"Crazy?"

"More than *funny*, at least." She picked up her brush again. "I don't know," she said. "Like Dad."

"Dad wasn't crazy. He just found greener pastures."

She looked at me. "Is that what Lawrence told you?"

"It's just what I know."

She turned back to the canvas. "You weren't even born."

I sat for a while longer, watching the robins in the oak. Lawrence, of course I do not know much about our father, and what I have gathered after these number of years comes almost completely from our mother and Darienne and Mrs. Silver; so perhaps it is unfair for me to believe it. Still, though, there is his evidence, as later there would be yours. You were so much his son in other ways, as I was our mother's, and in my surgical career I have come to understand the extraordinary breadth of what may be carried in the gamete.

After a few minutes I climbed back up the eave, and as I was stepping up into the dormer I turned around and saw that Darienne had painted me into her landscape, my shoulders and neck and the brown back of my head; a nice job of it, the shoulders curved in a pleasing way and the hair highlighted with pale brush marks so that it was more lively than my own. Yet it seemed to me it was not that far off from what I *could* have been; a more handsome version of the truth. As I climbed through the window, I looked back again; from there I had the same view of her as she had had of me, of her shoulders and her neck and her hair, of the darting wooden end of her brush, and what struck me suddenly was that she was the wisest and the most generous among us.

One day in the beginning of August, Zoltan called to say he had found something I'd be sorry to miss. We agreed to meet at the bluff late that afternoon. Waiting for him, I stepped over the wooden fence and walked to the edge of the cliff. This was the forbidden act of our childhood, standing on this part of the sandy, crusted edge above the river. Below me, the water slid relentlessly south, bubbling where the shore rifts met the main current. Now and then after the spring rains, huge chunks of earth would fall free from these parts, tearing loose and bumping down the steep slope into the river. The biggest ones, slabs half the size of a yard, would break up in the drop and crash in the shallow water like bombs. In the river a light cloud of mud would spread and move downstream, pale and thinning and angling in to shore.

Zoltan arrived as I stood there at the edge. He climbed over the fence and stepped next to me, the toes of his sneakers reaching over the end of the land. Clots of crusty earth dropped away below him.

"Careful."

He put his hands in his pockets and moved farther out until the balls of both feet were over the edge. "Don't be so scared of everything, Sellers."

"Who's scared?"

"You are."

"I've got a few things I want to do with the rest of my life."

"So do I."

"Okay," I said. "Okay."

The folds of his belly overhung his belt, and the corduroy legs of his pants shone where his thighs rubbed together as he walked. Suddenly I hated him.

"What are you thinking?" he said.

I flushed. I pulled a weed and threw it over. "You set those fires, Zoltan, didn't you?"

"What?"

"You burned the Melners' and the Salmons'."

"You're bonkers, Edward."

"I know you did."

He squatted at the edge and put his hands ahead into the air. "Well," he said, "what if I did?"

I dropped a clod over the edge. "You could have killed somebody."

"Listen, Sellers — you really think I'd do that?"

"Well, I don't know."

He stood. "I wouldn't kill anybody, man. I've got enough problems."

"How do you mean?"

"Forget it," he said, stepping back from the edge. "Come on; I'll show you something that'll open your eyes."

He climbed back over the fence and got on his bike. I considered staying there, but I hopped the fence and followed him. We rode along the palisade, his fat tires skidding in front of me and throwing out clouds of dust, his feet bucking on the gravel. A half mile south of town, where a path cut down to the river, we left our bikes on the shore and walked along the narrow beach. Out here the shore was cut in tiny bays, and at each opening a line of yellowish spume floated where the still inlet met the current. Bass made their nests in these waters. The beach and bottom were soft mud; shrubs grew from the bluff out past the water line, dying when the high water came. A few feet into the river, the trunks were pale gray and splintered, and the branches had no leaves. We walked. Zoltan stopped when we came around the bend of one of the inlets a mile south of town. He smiled thinly at me and told me to go ahead of him. I walked around the outcropping, and in the next bay, circled by shore shrubs and dead tree trunks, was the sunken motorboat we had seen at the beginning of the summer. Its hull tilted backward in the inlet so that the mildewed cabin canopy and the sharp bow rose at a steep angle, pointing into the deep water. The stern lay beached on the sandy reef where the spume floated; muddy water welled up over the engine. A rope held it there, tied from the struts to the tangled trunk of a bush on shore. In the water of the inlet I saw its whole pale shape beneath the surface, settled in the mud, the ghostlike hull throwing a long shadow along the bottom, and the small, dulled American flag floating upward from its slanted pole to rest on the surface.

"Amazing."

He was breathing hard behind me. "I found it a long time ago."

"You didn't tell anybody?"

He shrugged. "Who would I tell?" He walked past me and stood at the water line. "I just tied it up here." He took off his shoes and stepped into the shallow water, where puffs of mud spread up from his ankles. "I've been inside, too. There's something else."

He stepped back on shore and took off the rest of his clothing. The sun was below the trees now and the hull was dappled with its last light. I was going to be late for dinner, but I took off my pants and shirt and followed him into the warm water. He had produced a flashlight. We walked lightly, stepping straight up to keep the water clear, holding on to the rope that held the boat until we were at its side. I reached and felt the hull, which was covered with mossy fingers. The water rose past our chests.

Zoltan went under first. He thrashed a couple of times, kicked off the bottom, and flopped over the breaching rail into the hull. I followed. Under water I could see the white shapes of the benches, the dark carpet, and the bright, unfocused shine of the windshield. The beam of his flashlight appeared for a moment as he swept it around us, then disappeared. We came up for air and stood together on the slippery deck. "It's in back," he whispered.

I followed him along the narrow footway to the stern, where

the rope was tied. The bow reached into deeper water, and as we stepped toward the rear, the hull shifted and turned into the current. For a moment I felt it pulling us out, but then the rope caught and held us aground. We stood there, the boat rocking slightly beneath us; then Zoltan took a breath and dropped under again. I followed, and when I opened my eyes I saw him crouched on the deck. The sun was nearly gone, and in the silty water of the inlet I saw the pale shapes of his moving limbs and the magnified shine of the flashlight. He crawled toward the cabin. Something glinted, a row of fuzzy O's shining from his hand. I touched it: a chain. We moved along its silt-slicked length. The water was warm and lapped delicately around us. I surfaced for air, keeping my hand on the chain, and when I went down again he was pulling it, arm over arm, over the railing, until at its end he heaved, and a pale tangle flopped out of the darkness into the boat. He shone the light on its settling shape: it was the skeleton of a dog. I saw the huge eye sockets, the shortened snout, and the mossy shoulder blades aglint with tiny bubbles like fur. It tilted back and forth. He dropped the chain, and the flimsy shape followed it to the bottom of the boat, where the legs buckled into the bones of the haunch, and the tangled ribs spread out along the carpet.

I burst out of the water. Struggling for balance on the deck, I grabbed for the gunwale and gulped the mud-smelling air. Nausea rose in me, and I looked out at the dark horizon to quell it. I heard Zoltan surface, breathe, and go under; his knees and elbows and the wide, pleading front of his face shone in the flashlight's beam. The skeleton jerked up, then settled again into the hull. The flashlight went off. Only the skull showed now, a shining cone like a pop bottle under the water. I stood listening to the current out in the river. Then I dove over the side of the boat into the inlet and hurried back through the slimy bottom to the shore.

I sat down on a rock and squeezed the water from my hair. On my hands I could still feel the slickness of the chain, and at the edge of the river I rinsed them. I noticed that the rope holding the boat had shifted up along the bush where it was tied. I stood watching it. Each time Zoltan moved, it pulled taut and rode higher on the trunk; already it was near the tip.

As I stood there, Zoltan came up for air. He looked over at me, waved, and shouted, "I told you!"

"Told me what?"

"That I'd open your eyes." He spat a stream of water. "This beats some little fire, huh?"

"I guess so," I said.

He looked at me, expecting more. I turned sideways to him and nodded but didn't say anything, and when I looked again he had gone back under.

Standing there on the beach, Lawrence, I was aware that, just as you'd said, he and I had never really liked each other. Out in the cove, the canopy dipped below the surface and reappeared a few feet south. The rope suddenly slipped down into a fork of the bush. My heart skipped, but the knot pulled taut again.

As I watched the rope, I was aware of the deep differences between Zoltan and me. I would wait on the beach only until I was dry, then get dressed and ride home. But I knew Zoltan wouldn't. He would hide out there while the evening became night. He would crouch in the warm water of the hull, the skeleton turning before him in the current, holding him somehow, speaking to some hub of memory I would never know, darkening as he watched until at last it disappeared into the river.

Having seen the morbid cast of that face below the water, why did I approach Mr. Howland the next Saturday after Community Club and tell him about Zoltan? I have thought many times about my decision to do what I did; I have also thought about the certainty with which I later realized I was wrong. I told Mr. Howland I needed to talk, and after our meeting he waited for me in the hall. The overhead light gave his skin a violet cast, and when I saw his eyes I knew at once that he expected I had come about his daughter.

"It's not that," I said.

"Not what?"

"Not Lottie. It's something else."

Relief again moved through him, and he stepped toward me in the bright hall and sat on the concrete windowsill.

"It's not about Lottie; it's about Zoltan."

"Zoltan is a troubled boy."

"I know."

"What did you want to tell me about him?"

"It's important," I said.

He stood up from the windowsill, moved in front of me, and took my hand in his own like a priest. It was in such moments that his gentleness, which was occasional and powerful, showed itself most clearly, and although it is possible he was merely manipulating our confessions, Lawrence, I choose to believe that he cared about our troubles.

"He's been setting fires," I said.

His eyes widened. "What kind of fires?"

"He set the ones in those houses, the ones that burned — the Melners' and the Salmons'."

He let go of my hand. "How do you know?"

"I'm his friend. He burns things all the time."

"Are you sure?"

I thought of Zoltan crouched on the sunken hull. "I'm sure," I said.

He clasped my hand again. "I know this was difficult to tell me," he said, "but I want you to know it's a good thing that you've done, Edward. We're all grateful for this."

That afternoon, Zoltan asked me to come fishing with him, and as I rode behind him along the palisade I felt my second inklings of real affection for him, for the boy I had now betrayed. I felt affection for his ungainly efforts in the world, for his crass but honest dealings, and for the fate I now knew to be in store for him, which I imagined would bring him first to near ruin, and then, as our moral teachings seemed to dictate, to salvation — all by my hand. We rode on. He coasted ahead of me, his fishing rod extended past his handlebars like a lance. At the inlet, we stopped and looked down from the bluffs at the sunken boat, which now lay so close to shore it was nearly hidden by the slight slope of the cliffs. That afternoon we caught two bass, and when I left him in the evening to turn down the path toward home, I could see from a distance a patrol car parked in the driveway of his house.

What would the police have said to him? Would Sergeant Apt have treated Zoltan the way he used to treat you, sitting in the bright holding room across from him as though they were friends in all of this? Would he, for the moment, have only asked questions? That night I brought out my pinned boards of *Coleoptera* to examine, but I could not keep my thoughts on them, and, at last, contemplating my deed, I went downstairs to your room and told you what I had done.

You were reading *The Skeptic* and set it down when I had finished speaking. "Are you sure it was Zoltan?" you asked.

"I'm sure."

"Okay," you said, and picked up your magazine again, "then you did the right thing."

Lawrence, I was only fifteen, and entirely unaware of the caution an accusation required. The whole world, in fact, was still no larger for me than its familiar boundaries — our mother and Henry Howland and you, off in the distance ahead of me. Although I wonder now about the nature of deceit, about whether a deceiver must first convince himself of all the treachery he performs, I nonetheless believe that I never understood the consequences of what I said. The next night, the night after the police showed up at his house, Zoltan walked into the river.

He chose the stretch of beach where we used to watch the naked woman, and the following day they found him, held to the shallow bottom by the weight of the polished stones in the pockets of his pants. Our mother heard the news first and came out to the yard, where she put both her hands on my shoulders, then walked out to the bluff with me and told me while we sat and looked over the gentle water. " 'Whoever believes in me shall not perish,' " she whispered next to me, " 'but shall have eternal life.' " I lit a match and dropped it over the edge, where it spun in the drifts of wind and sailed out over the river. Zoltan, I ask you now for your forgiveness. My mother was wrong: I knew even then that you would have no eternal life. You had no faith when you were alive and no hope ever, I think, of any sort of paradise.

Zoltan was gone, and at first — as is common, I think, in many circumstances — I felt panic. As I sat on the bluff or at the kitchen table, as I lay in bed before sleep, a wild feeling would erupt in me: I was suddenly sure I had killed him. My heart exploded in my head and chest; the floor sloped away. And just as suddenly, the feeling would leave. I have since seen patients with this kind of reaction, and I tell myself that it is common. That Saturday, Mr. Howland gathered us along the beach and spoke about the hopelessness of Zoltan's act and the greatness of his sin — a sin, he said, that made our forgiveness a mark of the gentleness of our souls — while I stood on the sand and gripped my legs to keep from falling over. The morning was windless; he spoke standing ankle-deep in water that was calm as ice. Several times, I was sure, he looked right at me. When he finished, he asked us all to take off our shoes and stand in the inlet ourselves; we did so, and as the killing water lapped at my ankles, I was certain his gaze had found me again. I stepped on a patch of weeds and my heart leaped.

Did my words cause his sad end, Lawrence? I have concluded now that they did not, that I had acted with an abandon formed in ignorance, not in malice. Zoltan counted no friends except me among this group of barefoot teenagers standing six inches deep in the Mississippi River; if I was also his only traitor, then that is because I was the only one who had tried to show him kindness. We stood solemn and frightened as the eddies slid around us. Mr. Howland gave a short sermon about water as the source of life, and afterward he too became silent. I looked down at the river's placid bottom, then back to the beach along the inlet. My own footprints from the shoreline were already rounded over and disappearing.

Was he barefoot when he entered the water? The thought of preparation mystified me. Had he worn a windbreaker for the nighttime river breeze? Had he put his room in order, pushed in the small white chair to the small desk? Why had he polished the stones that were in his pockets? And what was the moment like when the water reached his mouth — did he close it? — and at his next step, when the river rose across the flat spread of his upper lip and touched his nostrils? These were his last remembrances of air and life. What a will the act required — the kind of will, it seemed to me, that might have led to greatness in another person; but Zoltan had no tie at all to splendor or excellence or greatness in the world. He was a fat kid with typical urges and a petty nastiness that declared itself with small crime — that was it, that was Zoltan. And I was his friend — or at least his companion — and now I had betrayed him.

I shuddered. When had he actually considered the idea of walking into the river? He knew its geography like none of the rest of us, knew its submerged trees and the sandbars that set up deep tugs of current. Had he spent time studying it for this very purpose? Or at the critical moment had he simply turned to the thing that had been with him the longest, that had surrounded his life and shaped it the way no person had? The low trees and the sun reflected in the water. I thought of his puffed face the night his car turned over. As I stood in the waveless inlet I wondered again whether his end had long been known to me.

I never cried for him — I hadn't cried in as long as I could remember — but in my bed that night I felt his absence all the way inside me, as a hollowness that may have been sadness but could just as easily have been fear. It was you, I believe, that I had become afraid of. Something within me was trying to make its way into the open; as if watching for its emergence, I stared out the dark window at the stars above the river. Soon I was asleep, and in the morning Zoltan was gone from the world in every sense I knew. After that night, my panic subsided, and I began to feel — especially when I thought of his mother, of her dark living room and the stiffened coif of her hair — I began to feel a loss within me that was harder and deeper than any I had ever known. This loss is still with me, Lawrence, although of course it has become smaller and almost unrecognizable. But I can feel it. With the passage of years it has turned, on Sunday mornings when I have stayed too long in bed, into a dread that cools my skin like approaching rain, and at night, if I am awakened and cannot fall asleep again, into the small gloom at the bottom of a glass of bourbon.

Within a few days I realized I had to make some effort to con-

sole Mrs. Morris. Our mother had baked a ham and brought it
over — most of the mothers had done something of the kind —
but as one day passed and then another, and Zoltan was now
five days in his grave, the sense took hold in me that my absolution would not be complete until I had gone over to the unlit
house and said something to Mrs. Morris about her son. And I
did, finally, one rainy morning; but as she sat across from me at
their yellow linoleum table, all she did was look beyond my
shoulder out the window. For a few, panicked moments, I wondered whether she knew that I had told the police about her
son. But then I gathered my calm, folded my hands on the table,
and told her that Zoltan had been unhappy only because certain
tricks of chance had turned out badly — I thought of his pink-
skinned fatness, his missing testicle, and the narrow, unpleasant set of his eyes, although of course I didn't mention these
things. And I told her, finally, that it was a mark of his kindness
that he had turned his hatred against himself and not against
the rest of us. This was the right thing to say, and she looked
down at me from the rainy window. It was an idea I had spent a
lot of time preparing, and the moment I gave it voice, sitting
across from her in a house I would never enter again, I felt for
the first time the ease with which treachery can comfort a man.

For a few days after Zoltan's death I was treated differently in
our family. Our mother, at the kitchen table and out back on
the porch, kept looking at me when she thought I was not paying attention; Darienne came to my room in the mornings, and
I would awaken to her whistling the Bellini concerto and whit-
tling reeds on my windowsill. Even you, Lawrence, seemed to
be listening to me the way you hadn't done before. You nodded
now when I spoke.

Then one day in August, with Zoltan only two weeks in his grave, I believe you decided you had had enough. How else am I to interpret what happened? That afternoon, Anita visited, and as we sat on the porch couch you came in and leaned against the frame of the screen door: you were wearing blue jeans and a yellow, button-down shirt that nipped at the waist and loosened at the shoulders. She moved away from me on the couch when we heard your steps on the stairs from the basement. Then you did a small thing, Lawrence — but I will never forget it: you leaned forward as you talked to us. "So, Anita," you said, hiding your hand behind you, shaking loose your shoulders, "how've you been?"

Then, over the next few days, you began paying attention to her. That was all; I cannot say I have evidence of anything more, but you must have been aware, especially in my circumstance, of what this did to me. In the past you had brushed by Anita, barely acknowledged her, spoken to her with the distantly attentive air of a schoolteacher, but you had never really looked at her. Now you were doing just that. How could I not notice? You nodded, and suddenly I saw a new view of your eyes. I cannot describe the difference, Lawrence, except that it made me realize I had never really known you. The heat and tenderness in them: I had to turn away.

"My brother's looking at you," I said to Anita when we were alone that afternoon in my room.

"You're not jealous, are you?"

"No, but watch out. My brother's a cad."

"He's not a cad."

"Yes, he is. He's trying to do something with those eyes of his."

"He's just being nice."

"Nice?" I said. I looked out the window, and as I did you moved suddenly into view below me, crossed the yard, and stood at its far end, gazing over the bluff. I watched you. When I turned around, Anita was watching also, and when she saw me, she lowered her eyes.

She left a few minutes later; I walked out back, past Mrs. Silver and our mother on the porch, and approached you where you stood facing out over the river at the bluff. I took a position beside you. I lit a match, tossed it into the divide, and we watched it sail until the updraft stopped it a dozen yards down along the side of the cliff and the flame extinguished in a tiny burst. You swiveled to look at the house behind us. I don't know what you were thinking, but it seemed to me that you had wronged me profoundly. "Lawrence," I said, "I know exactly what you're doing."

You laughed. "Good, Ed. Good." You faced the river again, tossed a stone from the edge, and watched it hit the cliff and bounce, hit again, and sail into the divide. You gave another laugh, and I felt a bolt of anger rise in me. Why were you laughing, Lawrence? I looked at you closely as you gazed down at the river. I don't know whether anyone ever sees the full arc of his life, but I believe you were trying to see your own right there. That was how you liked to look at things. You would have laughed, I think, at what you saw: perhaps this was what amused you. You felt no pity, after all — even for yourself. You tossed another stone, which flew past the promontory and sailed downward like a swallow. Then you picked up a handful of pebbles. Standing at the edge of the divide, you might have just seen the peak of your own existence, seen it right behind you, and although there was still nothing admitted between us, I believe you knew that what lay before you was your own descent.

"I know you, Lawrence. I know exactly what you're up to."

"That's right, Ed. You can see right through me."

"And what am I supposed to do about it?"

"I don't know, Ed. What do you think *I* would do about it?"

In one motion, you turned your back and threw the pebbles over your shoulder into the river. A cloud of sand drifted up from your hand like smoke. You appeared to consider something. Then you laughed again, this time full throated and with your mouth thrown open, before you started across the yard. Your chuckle rolled behind you on the breeze. Your back — the broad ball-and-piston seesaw of your shoulders — your back dipped and righted with each step. I could see your tense spinal muscles rolling over themselves like gears; I saw your strength, Lawrence, even through your shirt. Anger rose in me like flame. I took several quick steps toward you, and as you turned around I swung my fist — as you had always wanted me to, of course — at the angle of your brow; and it took so little for you to catch my blow as you did, with your bad hand, and hold my wrist up between us, like a trophy, and in an instant bend it backward so that my knee dropped to the grass before you let me go and went on walking, laughing still, across the yard and onto the porch toward the women.

I wonder how our lives might have been different if I had run more quietly behind you that day, if I had thrown my fist without the small grunt I now think I made in warning. A storm blew in later and as I put on my raincoat in the dark I was sure of the right I now had to harm you. I climbed out the window of my room into the rain drumming on the eave; from there I took hold of the porch column, where rainwater poured in a torrent, and lowered myself quietly onto the soaked floorboards. Inside the kitchen our mother was drying dishes. From the porch I crossed the yard to the shed and got out my bicycle.

Who can fathom the relations of brothers? I love you, Lawrence, and to this day I consider my life as tied to yours as to anyone else's in the world, to my wife's or to my son's, to our sister's or to our mother's. You are more a part of me than any of them. Yet there I rode: I pedaled harder and harder, speeding across the wet asphalt until my tires whined, pulling my hood down to shield my eyes from the wind-driven drops that soaked through the seamwork of my coat and ran in small streams down my neck and shirt. At the palisade the road ended and I skidded in the lane of gravel, stopping falls with my foot, then headed upriver, standing to pump the pedals, pushing the sluggish cut of the fat front wheel through the wet rocks. The rain fell harder. Black sheets cascaded around me, darkening the outlines of land and river. I rode and rode, panting, chilled by the night of storm, churning with anger that turned first to heat and then to sweat, mixing inside my pants and shirt with all the cold rain of heaven. At the Howlands' a light was burning. I could see it from the distance, and I pedaled harder, keeping my gaze to its glow. When I came nearer I saw him through the window, sitting at his desk, his head resting on his palm. I think, in the end, that he had grown tired from his trials but that he was no more than an ordinary man, Lawrence, exaggerated by all of us and made vindictive only by the tricks of your thought. As I watched, he lifted his head and gazed out into the rainswept air above the grass. He seemed to look through the row of bent trees, over the curving, soaked path, right at my approaching form.

At the house I propped my bicycle against the porch railing and went up the stairs to the door. An inside light shone weakly on the white columns and lit the entry, the curved windows, and the lion's paw door ornament; I waited, then pulled back the cool brass and knocked. I knew that Lottie slept on the first floor, not far from where I stood, and I imagined her shape pushing up the blankets the way they had in your room. I backed onto the lawn, where the rain now drummed in erratic torrents, small gusts of wind-driven drops that flew across the grass and thrummed on the floorboards of the porch. But between the bursts came a small silence. I moved back into that silence — three, four, five steps through the soaked greenery, the grass sinking under my sneakers like marshland.

The front door opened and Mr. Howland in a robe peered out. "Yes?" he said. "Yes? Hello?" His eyes without their spectacles squinted into the rainy mix of night colors. "Does someone need me?"

He looked out at the lawn where I stood. His eyes narrowed, passed left and right beyond me. I could see my own yellow sleeves shining in the pale cloudlight, but he squinted again and looked past.

"I have something else to tell you," I said.

"Who is that?"

"I want to tell you something I didn't tell you before."

"It's Edward Sellers," he said. He looked back and forth across the porch. "Where are you? Why don't you come into the house?"

"You're right," I said without moving. "It's me, Edward."

I retreated toward the back of the yard. "Edward Sellers," he said, "I know your voice. It's you." He pointed off to the left of me, into the woods. "It's you, Edward Sellers," he said, although I don't know why he kept saying this, because I was sure he had heard me answer him; and I don't know why at that moment I didn't tell him about you and Lottie, as I had come to do, and then walk away from his house into the rain, as I had intended, but instead pulled back my hood and climbed his steps, and stood with him in the darkened entryway to say the thing I had long known, although I could not have said how, but that came to me only as I stepped onto the slickened steps to

his porch: that it was you, Lawrence, and not Zoltan, who had
set the fires.

I rode home slowly. The rain had tapered to a mist that ob-
scured the trees and could as easily have been rising from
the ground as falling from the sky. I coasted most of the way
and pedaled the rest. It was near midnight, and I knew you
would be the only one awake. When I entered your room,
you were lifting dumbbells on your bed, holding your forearm on the downstroke until it shook, counting the beats
while a flush spread up your neck and across your face. I tried
to look calm. "Lawrence," I said at last, "I told about the
fires."

You lifted your arm to midposition and held it. A drop of
sweat rolled down your face. "Take it easy, champ."

"I told Mr. Howland about them."

You moved your arm to three-quarters position and held your
chin down to watch it shake. "That's why your friend's in the
river, champ."

"No, Lawrence, I told him *you* set them."

The dumbbell moved to midposition again. "You told him
what?"

"That you set them."

"You told him that *I* set them?"

"Yeah."

You moved the dumbbell to your bad hand. "You're lying."

"No, I'm not."

"Why'd you do that?"

"I don't know." You put down the weight and stood, and I
went to the window. After a time I looked back at you. You

were leaning over the dresser examining your teeth, opening your lips and leaning back so that the dark roof of your mouth showed in the mirror, and when you saw me looking, you yawned and ran your fingers through your hair.

"Come here, Ed," you said. "Stand next to me. What do you see?"

I moved behind you at the dresser. "Your shoulder mostly."

You opened your mouth again and looked inside. "You know what I see, Ed? I see the same person. You and me, we're the same old bastard Dad was." You laughed, then pulled the belt from your pants and held it through the four-pointed, brass star in its buckle. "That's an important thing to know, Ed. You do know it, don't you?"

"Not necessarily, Lawrence."

You made a motion toward the ceiling with your arm, which I followed with my eyes, and in an instant you had knocked me to the floor and pinned me like an insect. You held me to the carpet and cocked back the belt in your fist, and I saw for an instant in the buckle over your shoulder the depth of our life-long rivalry — I saw this so clearly, Lawrence — and I turned my head and tried to hide my face in the carpet; I felt your arm rear back and your muscles tense, and for the briefest instant I was resigned, because it gave me relief to imagine the hot cut of the buckle across my cheek and the welling, cloudy pain of it; I deserved it, after all. But then I felt your grip release, and the blow didn't come, and I turned and watched you lower your elbow first, then your wrist so that the belt lay across my shoulders, then your head, so that when I rolled away from you and stood, your face was hidden in the carpet, and I think now that if you had only hit me that night we might not have found ourselves, these years later, where we have, because I believe I could have forgiven you for that; I believe if you had only swung at me, our relations would be clear to this day; but as it stands I have come this far in my life not sure of what has passed between us, of which of us has hurt the other more, and — I might as well say this, Lawrence — I suspect that this is part of why I have done to you what I have.

You rose from the floor. Your voice, when you finally spoke, was uninflected. "Will you take me to the bus, Ed?"

"Where are you going?"

"California."

"California?"

"It's time I got out of here."

I will never understand how you left as easily as you did that night, packing a single duffel in the short time I stood there in your room, leaving everything else behind so that it was months before I actually understood you had gone forever. I helped you collect your things: the violence I had glimpsed in you had vanished so completely that the fear in me was gone as well. You said nothing to Darienne or to our mother. I drove you to the station before dawn, while they still slept, and hugged you across the shoulders at the door to the westbound local as the driver slid your duffel into the hold, and then I watched you board the bus in the darkness. It would take you to Davenport, Iowa, and there you would catch the cross-country express. You rode out of our lives like a stranger, Lawrence. Did you leave us so easily because you had never felt a part of our family? I suppose this was the cause and the price of the strength you always had — the nasty, hard, solitary conviction that lay at your center like a black rock. I watched the bus until it disappeared.

The next afternoon the police came. Our mother called me down to the front hall, and she led us to the steps above your basement room. She held her arms tightly across her chest, and her voice, when she asked me if I knew where you had gone, was full of the tightness I had almost forgotten. Sergeant Apt was accompanied by a young patrolman, who shook his head and looked at his shoes. I didn't answer immediately; we shuffled down the stairs, our mother descending ahead of us and opening the door to your room. When we were all huddled inside, I answered: "He went to Corinth for the day."

They looked around. This must be why you had packed so little, so that it would seem you had indeed left only for the afternoon. The criminal calculation to your thinking sent a chill through me when I recognized it; although in the moments before I had answered our mother's question, in the time it took me to move down the stairs and enter your room, I myself had been equally calculating: my answer gave your bus a chance to reach the border. I did that for you, Lawrence.

They returned the next morning, and when they saw that your bed had not been slept in — I considered rumpling the sheets, but didn't — the young officer glanced at Sergeant Apt. They came again in the afternoon, and by then the sergeant's face had taken on a gray sadness, so that as he looked around your room and then came up the stairs and stood examining our house from the yard, I saw him once again as a friend in all of this, as a man who had always wished you well. I almost told him the truth.

How did you expect our mother and Darienne to react? When a day passed, and then another, and finally I wrote a note in your back-slanting print and told them I had found it in the drawer of my desk — "I have gone to try my luck in the world" — our mother did not weep. I suppose that for a long time she had been expecting this kind of ending; she had experience, after all, with sudden departures. As she went about her life, she changed only in the smallest ways: she went back briefly to the Bible, but this did not last; she ate less and soon became quite thin; she drank her tea without speaking.

It was Darienne who felt your loss most deeply. After that

day, Lawrence, she became another person — almost the same way you had, three years earlier. I have begun to think, in fact, that this is a trait in our family, these sudden, calamitous reappraisals of life. It was what our father had done — and I have wondered if it will ever happen to me.

When I remember our sister, I think the change may have done her good. It was as if the world, which for her had never been much larger than our house, our family, her music, and the still lifes she painted, now took on new shape and dimension. Calls began coming for her well into the night; eating her breakfast alone on the porch, she assumed a distant, brooding air; her canvases lay propped against window ledges and baseboards in the house until dust covered them and first the blues, then the reds, faded in the sunlight. One day in her sketchbook I found pages and pages of pencil portraits she had made, starting with drawings of you as a child — I recognized the photographs they were taken from — progressing through renderings of what you looked like now, and ending with several eerie versions of what she imagined would become of you — this must be a standard artist's exercise — so that the last ones were of what our sister thought you would look like in your coffin.

The week after you left, Mrs. Silver and our mother and I went to hear Darienne play the Bellini concerto. She had gone off that morning without speaking to us, her shoes in a bag, her black performance dress rolled inside a damp towel. Shortly after we took our seats in the auditorium, she came out onstage with two boys who carried the kettle drum, her eyes now dark with mascara. The players around her started tuning their instruments — violins and violas, cellos, woodwinds — the jumble of sounds rising and falling without a line for any of us to follow. And suddenly I heard Darienne. The opening notes of the Bellini rose up over the metallic jingle and clap of the other players, coming out to me as pure as water. For the first time I realized their beauty.

She stopped. I looked up, and she had removed her reeds and was sucking them. The other instruments kept tuning, the drawn-out notes rising and falling around the pitch. Mrs. Silver poked me. "Did you hear that?"

"You mean Dary?"

"Yes."

"She's good, isn't she?"

"Good heavens, we never knew that, did we? Our Dary."

I thought of her, of the deliberate, plodding scales she practiced in her bedroom or the front room of our house, of the light from the front yard coming in through the thin curtains and setting the oboe's metal keys glowing. At home she went up and down scales, fiercely, so slow as to get them perfect, the spit-soaked reeds tiring her after an hour. Then she went to the sink and ran cold water over the inside of her lips, where small white vesicles were raised from the vibrations. She liked to show them to me, proud that she had caused herself injury; but they only made me hate more the sound of her playing. I had never liked it. The notes, so many times repeated, lost all musical quality; long ago they had become just Darienne practicing — not things of beauty, not music, just exercises. I tolerated them, thinking about other things until their climb and fall were lost to me, and when I was back in my own room or outside in the yard, her practicing actually seemed like silence. Now, though, with the rest of the players tuning, the sound of her oboe lifted up and came out to me, rushing down like rain to fill the riverbed it had cut in my memory.

The lights went out. The audience quieted and the musicians

stopped tuning, and then Mr. MacFarquhar, fat in his black suit, fatter than anyone I had ever seen, came onstage. The players sat still. I looked at Darienne, now lit on one side by the stage lights, her hair pulled back, her shiny black dress, which I had last seen rolled into a towel, changing her suddenly into a woman. The lights had been filtered with colored plastic so that her skin took on a carrot-colored depth. Not just her clothing and her complexion but her concentration, the dark, upturned lids of her eyes and the tautness of her cheeks, waiting to play, made her seem *needless*. That was what unexpectedly wounded me: with you gone I felt suddenly unimportant to her, as if I had had my chance but that she — sitting up there with the reed tip in her mouth, her face tilted down toward the music on the stand in front of her and Mr. MacFarquhar on the podium — she had now gone on without us.

She adjusted the reed between her lips. Mr. MacFarquhar raised his arms. They came down, and the music started, the first-row girls swinging into their violins with their elbows high, like batters, and the boys one row back coming in a beat later, after they were sure. The music rose and fell. Suddenly the others hushed, Darienne stood, and, gazing past us into the distant seats, played through the sequence I had heard hundreds of times before. I heard her breaths, the same quick, strained inhalations, panting and throaty, that came from our living room. Her melody built to a crescendo, then quieted, and the other instruments joined in again. Each time a solo was to arrive, she readied several bars early. She drew the reed to her lips, removed it, and drew it back again. Bobbing her head, she counted off the beats, then stood to play, rocking forward, her thin shoulders pulling in on themselves and the oboe moving up and back in the air in front of her.

After the concert, after the applause and Mr. MacFarquhar's

second bow, and then one taken by Darienne at the podium, we waited for her by the stage door. Our mother stood silently with her head bowed.

"Dary," I said when I saw her, "you were wonderful."

She looked at me.

"Perfect," said Mrs. Silver.

"Exquisite," said our mother.

"You were great," said Mrs. Silver. "You really, truly were."

"That was for Lawrence," she said.

Our mother cocked her head. "We all wish he could have heard it, honey."

"He did hear it," said Darienne.

"That's a nice thought," said our mother.

"It's not just a thought," said Darienne. Then she turned away from us — our oily-haired, droop-shouldered sister — clasping the oboe case to her small breasts, her black dress picking up reflected light, her eyes sad with mascara, smiling queerly at the curtain, smiling like someone we had never seen before.

You know all about what happened next, Lawrence. On the Saturday after I left you at the bus, six days after you were supposed to be in California, late at night, when most of the town was asleep, another house burned. I first saw the light of it through my window, where I lay looking out at the low cumulus clouds and the sprinkling of stars. To the north, yellow-red touched a cloud bottom, and by the time I had dressed and was a hundred yards up the palisade on my bicycle, I realized the fire was far away, beyond the white luminescence of the tool plant and past the edge of town. I rode past the Burrows' and the deNiords', beyond the marina and onto the eroding section of cut cliff where no houses stood; I pedaled past the empty land until the flames themselves jumped into view, retreated behind the treetops, then jumped again, until, coming around a bend in the shore, I saw the burning house: it was the Howlands'.

The four carved columns were gone. The overhanging second floor leaned over the porch, and the whole burning front section was about to fall in on itself. Along the hallway where Lottie had wheeled toward us almost two months before — had all this happened that fast? — smoke fled up from the windows, boiling into the sky. Three firetrucks stood out front, and through the smoky rear windows of the kitchen I saw the men inside. People stood at the edge of the lawn. Where was Henry Howland? Where was Lottie? I dropped my bicycle and moved to the lawn, where each step took me into smokier air, dryer air, air so filled with heat it seemed to have been electrified. I saw Charles Sankowich, Philip Bronson, Mrs. Morris, Mr. deNoird; I saw most of the Community Club, huddled at the head of the driveway; but were the Howlands still inside? Were they asleep in the fire? Flames leaped through the porthole windows upstairs. Then, stepping back toward the elms and the cool air they sheltered, I saw them, Lottie and her father, at the edge of the crowd, looking up into the burning shell of their house.

In an instant I was back on my bicycle. I cut through the low trees and back to the sliding gravel path along the river. Having seen the flames, I now felt among them. They threw me forward, stood me up at the pedals so that even in the moonless night I shot forward on the path. The tires skidded on rocks, cut back in the dust, and threw me homeward, then past home, and then out of town again, south past the bluffs and into the sloping land around Animal's Castle. There, I finally dropped my bicycle. Blades of grass rose above my head; they bent forward in the darkness, showing silver and black. Behind me, not just the clouds but the sky itself had grown yellow with smoke, so that one whole half of the world looked larger, practically sun-lit, possessed of its own light, a glow that diminished the small black horizon in front of me. I walked in its queer, shifting shadow. I passed toward the river once, stopped, and passed back. By now I could see the dense tufts of stems and the black earth between them, but no matted grass showed among the side-bent stalks.

"Lawrence," I said into the warm night. "It's you, Lawrence. I know it is."

I knew that you were watching me, Lawrence; I could always sense your presence. And I knew what had happened: you had got off the bus, hidden in the woods along the river, and then waited for the right moment. I passed through the length of the meadow another time, then back again, while the smoke blew high above me as though particles of light had been borne into the wind. But in their eerie cast I saw nothing, no clue or trace, no human form. I climbed into the lowest branches of one of the oaks, but in the sea of grass before me I saw no movement. I sat there a long time. "Lawrence," I said at last into the gentle wind, "I'm not a traitor." I listened to the insects and the distant sirens. "I'm not a traitor, Lawrence."

If you were there, why didn't you come out? Though you may not understand this, I believe that in those days I meant you no harm. I wanted only to help you. But when I climbed out of the oak and passed through the field again and again, I saw nothing, and at last I climbed out of the grass and walked to the river. I sat there and gazed at the dull heavens turning in the current. At that moment, Lawrence, next to the water, I was still with you. I knew the hard, uncontainable rage of your soul, that nothing could ever heal a wound like that. I knew that others would forsake you; they already had. From that day forward the world would set itself irrevocably against you, would haunt and thwart you, would keep you distant from its bounty — I knew that, Lawrence. But right then, more than anything else, I wanted to stay by your side. Standing next to the river, at that age when I first began to see our lives not as inevitable but as they really were, as changeable and frail, I thought I would never leave you.

III

CALIFORNIA

WHEN YOUR BUS FINALLY moves away from the station, I start the Land Cruiser and suddenly notice what I had meant to show you all along: the small, faded Yellow Nightshine beetle encased in the plastic ornament on my key chain. I never did find it, Lawrence — I looked and looked — but the year I finished my residency I finally bought it; we could have laughed at that. Now, as your coach changes lanes and pulls ahead, I toss the key chain's pendant in my fingers and wish I had shown it to you — a wish so sharp it startles me. I pull into the light traffic and drive behind you again as far as the freeway. The windows of the coach are dark and I cannot see you, though I look. I wait at the ramp while the bus climbs ahead of me. The lights blink off as the driver downshifts for the acceleration, then come on bright as he heads over the summit and into the empty lanes toward Nevada. But I do not follow. Abraham barks once as the lights disappear.

I turn the Land Cruiser around and head back the other way. I do not know the story of your life anymore, Lawrence; I do not know what has happened to you in the years since you left us. I cannot even guess. I do know, however, that it is not what has happened to me. Where should a man's loyalty lie? Where can he turn if the good fortune of his own life feels, as mine does, undeserved, yet is there nonetheless? Should I have taken you in? At home now my son sleeps in sheets with bears on them, and as I drive I picture the shine of his untroubled cheeks by nightlight.

Few cars are on the road. I know that your life has not turned out the way you once thought it might — the way *we* once thought — that the unraveling dilapidation of character that I know was in our father has struck you too, so that you woke one morning — one month of mornings, one year of them — disappointed, as though everything solid had belonged to your past and would not ever be there again; I know this, Lawrence. The disappointment, I imagine, turned one morning to a memory, and in a month or year to even less than a memory, and in more time still it became not a disappointment but your character itself. I can see in the languid workings of your mouth and jaw — this is the privileged knowledge of my profession — that you have taken medicines to ease your trouble.

A few days after you disappeared from Blue River for good, they found your camp in the woods near the Howlands' house. They found your gas cans — they had come from our garage — your little cookstove, and your meager leavings. But even now, I cannot explain what had convinced me before that, climbing the rain-slickened stairs to Henry Howland's porch, that you were the arsonist. The town was shocked at your crimes, but I was not and never have been. I have learned, Lawrence, not only from you but from the profession of medicine as well, that the human imagination is capable of profound deception and utterly inexplicable action: I have felt with my hands the dozen swallowed knives in the stomach of a teenage boy; I have seen a woman who plucked out her own eyeball. What you did, by comparison, seems straightforward: you destroyed the monuments of your past.

I know most of your old secrets, Lawrence. I have surmised, for example, that Lyna Melner's baby was yours, that despite all your denials it was in fact you who had made her pregnant, long ago. I believe we all knew that; we had simply let the fact of it disappear, like a sinking boat. I once tried to locate Lyna, because for a time I believed that she might settle the matter; but after I failed to find her, I realized that she probably would not. Only recently, however, did I understand that what our mother had said to me all my life — "you'll end up like Lyna Melner" — was not, as I had always thought, a warning that I would wreck my own life, but that *you* would wreck it.

I wonder why our mother thought the two of us were so different, when it had always seemed to both of us that we were alike. I know from the letter you sent me after you left that you believed our mother had always *wanted* us to be different; and, to be fair, there may be some truth in this. Once, years later, when I was visiting home from medical school, I had several drinks with her in a restaurant and she told me something extraordinary. She had, by then, developed a slight limp, was living alone in Wisconsin, and had settled into the earliest forms of the restrained bitterness that has since taken root in her bearing. She had become, I think, finally and fully angry at our father. We went to the dockside restaurant that had recently opened for the motorboat crowd living in the new developments down the river, and we ordered vodka cranberries on the deck. We talked about my future in medicine — I was at the time deciding between general surgery and ophthalmology — and about Darienne's life in St. Louis, where she was already married and teaching music. Our mother ordered another drink, and in the time the waiter took to bring it, our conversation faltered: I think we both realized that we had not talked about *you*.

When her drink arrived she sipped it and then said, without warning, "Grace enters through our wounds." She drank again, looked over the river through the deck rail, and said, "When I was pregnant with your brother, I was going through a period when I hated your father." She shook the ice in her glass. "I hated him. Can you imagine what it's like to hate the man you married? He just changed one day," she said. "One day when we'd been married three years, something inside him just went haywire — " She looked at me. "Do you want to hear this? He went crazy, really; he just turned into another person." She held the empty glass to her lips. "He turned into a hateful person. I hated him. Try to imagine what that's like."

I waited a moment. "I can't imagine."

"I used to drive around sometimes after work and look at the embankments along the highway. There were a lot of bridges around because of the access roads, and each one had a concrete embankment. Bad accidents happened at those embankments. I was just getting big with Lawrence then. I used to drive at the edge of the lane to look at them. I knew which ones didn't have guard rails."

"Why were you doing that?"

"I wanted — " She laughed. She didn't finish her sentence, but I now know, of course, what she was referring to. "When I was pregnant with Lawrence," she said instead, "all I could think about was hate. That's what happened to his hand."

Her eyes had moved off to the side. "The doctor gave you tranquilizers, Mom," I said. "The tranquilizers were teratogenic. His hand was from the tranquilizers."

"No, it wasn't," she said. "My own hate made that hand." She set down her glass. "That's where it came from."

So you see, Lawrence, when I pull over to a rest stop now and read your letter again after all these years, it is difficult for me not to see you in a half light of absolution. Sleeping trucks rumble in the night.

August 14, 1975

Edward —

By the time you read this I'll be gone, as you probably know. As you probably also know by now, we won't see each other for a while. I'm going to have to do some hiding. That's what I'm doing now, hiding, and I'm wishing I was in my little room. You've probably never thought of it as little, because I know that you think many of the things I do are *big*. You thought I was a big fighter, for example, and a big lover. But you will see one day that the little apartment I lived in is exactly that — *little*. I had a bookshelf and the weights and the bed. A few girls visited me there, but not as many as you think. Time is going to change the things you see. I remember as a child, before you were born, going with Dad (have I ever said that word to you: *Dad?*) to the state fair and riding a ferris wheel that was as high as a building. At the top I was terrified because I could look all the way across the river into Minnesota. The metal struts holding the chairs were about as wide as my fingers. I didn't go back there for ten years, maybe, but one year I did. There was a new ferris wheel by then, and it wasn't nearly as big as the old one. We rode it and the ride was short. We went up and paused a minute at the top, then came down. There were none of the old views all the way to Minnesota, and none of the whistling wind and cold of the old one. I was disappointed. After I came down I talked to the operator, who was an old guy, and he told me that the same ferris wheel had been there for twenty years.

So, Edward, things are going to change. One day you're going to have to decide about me. You're going to have to decide how much of what you thought about me was in your imagination. I used to fight. That's something you'll remember. (You'll remember because *you* didn't. If you had ever split another boy's cheek with your knuckle, if you'd ever felt the non-feel of a landed punch, the way the nerves in your hand and arm just go dead for a second, the way it feels no different than running your hand through a swimming pool, then you wouldn't remember my fighting. But that wasn't the way you were.) You're going to remember all this because you didn't do it yourself. One day, it might even seem like it was you and not me who went out at night with a stick in your back pocket and a chain in your hand.

You didn't have to do that, though. *I* had to. Mom wanted me to punch people, so I did. (I was behaving, too.) Does this seem crazy to you? I made them bleed. That's what she wanted. (If you don't believe this, you're not going to believe anything.) You know as well as I do who she was after. Did you know that the nicest she ever was to me was when I came home with a cut or when I had a broken bone in my hand, a "boxer's" fracture. (What's that bone called, Ed?)

Am I mad you told Howland? No, Ed, I'm not. I knew you would. I'm just glad he knows who hit him. I'm glad he doesn't think it was old Zoltan. As Dad would have said, "It was time to pay the piper."

A lot of big talk from your philosophical brother, right? I have never understood faith in the slightest. But I don't want to, either; there's enough to understand in the back yard. That's the thing, Ed: We Don't Know Anything Yet.

That's why I can't imagine faith is any closer to understanding than science is.

When you read this I'm going to be gone. You probably
think I'll be with a girl. I'd like to be, that's true — the window open and everything, heading west. But that's another
thing you exaggerate about me. I think you believed I had
some special power. I know that, because people told me
what you said about me. Ed, nobody has special power. I
was just hungry. I was starving. It was the only moment in
my life when I wasn't sinking, you know, but actually rising, out of gloom, out of something — I can't put my finger
on it — out of the apartment downstairs while up in the
house you all walked around. You touched each other. I
could hear you all, your footsteps coming together on the
ceiling. Mom kissed the top of your head. She put her hand
on Darienne's ears. Downstairs I could hear that.

It's getting dark. When I think about my old life, I think
about how I used to listen to your steps above me in my
apartment. Did you know that yours are different from
Mom's or Darienne's? Yours are lighter and more even.
(It's like you've practiced your walking.) Dary stumbles
around, like she has a peg leg or something. That's about
right for her, isn't it? I guess I love you, although I don't
know what that means exactly. We have the same blood.
We have the same thoughts. That's probably enough.
When I was teaching, I always wished I had one student
who understood as much as you do.

L.

(P.S. Yes, you were a traitor.)

Abraham barks once and I put the Land Cruiser in gear again.
At night here, even on the freeway, the air smells of cypress,

and as I drive toward home I open the window. Behind me Abraham is still nervous. He paces door to door, and when I turn around to look at him he arches suddenly and leaps up next to me; in the darkness I reach across and touch the soft fur below his ears. And though I would like to say that I do not close my eyes, I *do*, in fact, and for a few seconds I do not let them open. The car runs downhill on the curve as I listen to the hum of tires and the squeaking of the suspension, and it is as clear to me now as it has always been, as I feel the road bank up beneath me, why I do this: I have known, I think, for years.

I know as well that a single act can hardly change a life, that all cures are slower than we hope, but I take this exit anyway, here amid this unfamiliar land. Abraham is barking again. I am probably doing a foolish thing, but you cannot be more than a few miles ahead of us, Lawrence, on a road that is near to empty, and I say out loud that I will give myself the chance to change my mind again as I drive; and this is enough to convince me to turn and follow you at least a little farther, so that as I pull the car off the freeway and circle underneath it, and as I come up again on the other side, on the inclined branch of cloverleaf that leaves us at the top along a line of reflected light, beautiful as a runway, I know somehow that I am heading for a time of difficulty in my life; yet I have the hope that I will find the courage to fetch you, and that we will find a way to end this, you and I, so that peace will come to us; and as I top a hill and see in front of me your bus's distant taillights and the blinking vista of these sleeping towns, I feel the sudden, ebullient, etherous opening in my chest that is faith, perhaps, or God, or blinding light.

The author is grateful to a number of people for help with this book: Pixie Apt, Chard deNiord, Ellie Dwight, Alex Gansa, Richard Green, Maxine Groffsky, Jonathan Howland, Anne Lamott, Rosina Lippi-Green, Deborah Rogers, Barbara Schuler, Martin Cruz Smith, and above all, John Sterling.